MW01181042

The Blood of Balor Woods

A.J. Zanders

AuthorHouse™
1663 Liberty Drive
Bloomington, IN 47403
www.authorhouse.com
Phone: 1-800-839-8640

First published by AuthorHouse 12/08/2010

ISBN: 978-1-4520-7191-6 (sc)
ISBN: 978-1-4520-7192-3 (e)

Printed in the United States of America

authorHOUSE®

Acknowledgments:

I want to give a huge thank you to everyone who helped me create this book. I could not have done it without them. *Authorhouse* of course, without their services you wouldn't be holding this book. My husband Josh for his support, my father for taking the time to tell everyone about it, my Aunt Susanne who encouraged me and edited the book with the little amount of free time she has; my father in law Ben for proof reading; my friends, Sharon and Kat (who initially took the time to read it), Elizabeth (for her outstanding inside illustrations), Cheryl, Alisha, Jerry, Melody and Marlin (for their support), Victor (for his amazing job on the cover), Patrick (for letting me use him as a model for the cover. He did a wonderful job). Toni and Shannon for the final proofread Also I want to thank all those who read my fanfictions as Koi_kami for your encouragement. I would not have stepped out on my own had it not been for your gracious reviews. And to every reader who picks up this book. Thanks to all of you.

- A. J. Zanders -

A.J. Zanders

Character guide:

Isaac: Wood sprite prince, his father is the water sprite king his mother the priestess of the wood sprites.

Sam: An orphan girl with a talent for growing plants trying to survive on her own in the city

Wisteria: An old sprite who teaches Isaac the ways of the forest

Lumeria: Princess of the water sprites

Renlacir: King of the water sprites and Lumeria's brother

Marco: Sicilian drug lord who uses Sam's talents to his advantage

Lewis Valentino: Sam's only reprieve while working for Marco

Greek brother's Jimmy and Johnny: Rival drug dealers

Cary: An elderly woman whom Isaac shares a close relationship with.

A.J. Zanders

Prologue

(Two and a half centuries ago)

Goose flesh prickled along her arms. The gossamer silk draping her tiny frame did nothing to block the frigid December air. Despite her discomfort she did not reach up to rub her arms for warmth. Stubbornly, she pushed forward through the dense woods escorted by the resonating sound of bells ringing atop their staffs. The rhythm of their chimes matched the shaman's steps keeping stride behind her. As they neared the cliff the rush of water drowned out the sounds of the bells. Below, the forest opened to a cloud of mist concealing a wall of granite and lime; a mass of milky water spilt forth from high above. Rowan stopped as her feet sunk into the cool damp earth, mud squished up between her toes.

The rush of water grew louder and she could feel the mist on her bare arms sending more goose bumps up her spine. One of the village's shamans tried to push her forward. "Stop do you not feel it?" the elder's voice commanded. The young shaman turned to his superior. "Feel what?" The village elder stepped past his apprentice to stand only an inch from the edge of the cliff. Rowan shivered beside him. The elder shouted into the mist, "Renlacir, we have brought the girl; please show yourself."

A high pitched whistle resounded from behind the waterfall. The mist began to thicken; the droplets started clinging to each other like mercury. Something solid formed from within the mist. A girl with long sliver hair and celestial blue eyes appeared before them and the mist was gone, "Salutations forest kinsmen my brother is waiting"

Rowan took a step back from the strange girl who just appeared out of nowhere. Elder Sequoia placed his staff behind Rowan blocking her retreat. "Princess Lumeria…is this woman of your prophesies?" Lumeria turned her piercing blue eyes on the veiled woman and stepped in closer. With the elder's staff at her back and the cliff at her left Rowan could only stand there as the girl approached. She could feel a cool draft coming from the girl's skin. Icy blue met emerald green and the girl smiled. "Please allow me to see."… The girl took a step closer until there was no more room between them. Lumeria's body seemed to break down as she touched Rowan's skin; then the princess was absorbed into her pores. She felt the chill of ice as the girl merged with her own body. Her fingers stiffened and her body shivered until she fell to her knees. Tears ran down her cheeks. Her escorts gathered around in anticipation. "Priestess?"

Rowan's eyes opened as shining blue jewels. Her voice was soft and pure. "She is the one, a union of her flesh and my brother will yield the heir of the forest you seek…" Her eyes widened and her face froze before her body began to convulse in fits of sobs. She choked on the tears. "He will save your people, but he will perish in unholy flames if he becomes the next guardian of the forest…AHH!…STOP IT, YOU WITCH! GET OUT OF MY HEAD!" Rowan pressed her fist into to her temples the pain was unbearable. She struggled to regain control of her body from the water sprite princess. The other wood sprites did not expect this from the woman they reluctantly called 'priestess'. One of the shamans tried to hold her still, "No you mustn't fight it; this is your destiny…"

Her body slipped free of his grasp like an eel, than began to move on its own toward the falls. Rowan fought with the water sprite princess still inside her. Uncontrollably her feet carried her closer and closer to edge of the cliff. -*Let me go child I did not agree to this you cannot determine my fate*! *It is your destiny to consummate with my brother, he is waiting for you*.- The two sharing the same body and limbs plunged into the milky pool below.

The Blood of Balor Woods

A.J. Zanders

Ch. 1

"A child of mix blood will be born"

The concrete was cold, hard and smooth under Isaac's feet. It was nothing like the uneven, muddy ground of the forest. Here the ground was gray or black and the walls surrounding him were either dingy, red brick or cold, silver steel. The only animal he passed on the way to the corner was an old bony grey cat that was missing an ear as well as most of its fur. Stopping in the alley Isaac knelt down and called to it, "Here puss, puss...come here I won't hurt you." Flattening its ears it stared back warily at the boy, uncertain whether to stay or run. When Isaac locked eyes with the mangy animal it relaxed instantly and waltz over, rubbing up against his leg. Frowning at the poor creature's appearance, Isaac reached down petting its ratted fur. Every cell in the feline's body reacted to his touch; mending and rejuvenating flesh that had gone missing. By the time Isaac had stroked the cat's tail its entire body was healed. It parted with a grateful mew and trotted down the street. Watching the cat leave, Isaac was happy he could help it, but he had to admit; Wisteria was right about one thing. The forest was prettier and seemed kinder to its inhabitants, than the city. However; there were certain things the forest didn't provide. One was Lyna's delicious oatmeal cookies and there certainly weren't any arcades in the forest, but most important of all was Cary. She was in the hospital several blocks away. She was the closest thing he had to a mom since Wisteria had made it quite clear that she was not. Cary didn't treat him like Wisteria did. She always looked happy to see him and gave him presents. Wisteria, on the other hand always seemed angry with him. She was always giving him tasks to perform and would yell at him if he did not do it perfectly. Just because she was the only other wood sprite left, didn't give her the right to treat him so harshly. A day hadn't gone by that she didn't remind him of the importance of his training. Isaac was tired of feeling pressured to learn everything there was about the forest. Wisteria had told him hundreds of times that he was the only one who could save their people, but why should he care?

Stepping up to the curb; Isaac stared down at his ratted sneakers where several dandelions were pushing their way through the cracks in the sidewalk. As he stood there a thought bubbled up and burst in his mind; he had never met "their people". Why should he work so hard to save people he didn't know? Cary however, was flesh and blood, and that's what was important to him, not some invisible ancestors.

Soon the light changed at the crosswalk and the cars resumed speeding down the street. A gathering of puffy sleeves and tweed coats began pushing and shoving at the corner. The commuters did their best to fit at the edge of the sidewalk; no one spoke. They all just stared

straight ahead waiting for the signal to turn from a
hand to a silhouette. A woman in a long flowered
dress, an oversized vinyl green handbag hanging
loosely from her shoulder walked up and stood
next to Isaac. Looking up at the woman's freckled
face, he smiled; she didn't notice. He wiggled a
hand free from his long faded green sleeve and
bent down pretending to tie his shoes. He slipped
his hand past his sneaker and dug a finger into a
crack. Pulling the oversized sweater over his knees
with his free hand; he made sure no one could see,
and then he whispered something inaudible. A
dandelion pushed its way up stretching higher
and higher toward the sun. It slithered up the
length of the woman's floral dress, and curved
around where her handbag was resting against
her side. It dove through an opening in the zipper.
The woman felt a tug and looked down; a small
boy with spiky brown hair sticking out of a green
hood greeted her with a warm smile. "Ma'am did
you drop this?" She reached out smiling taking the
small tube from the boy's outstretched hand,
"Thank you sweetheart" Slipping the small silver
tube back into her purse she turned her attention
to the light across the street. Once the signal

changed, the crowd ushered the woman across; leaving the small boy standing on the corner waving goodbye.

As soon as he was alone Isaac looked down in his hand and smiled. He sorted through an empty gum wrapper, a loose button, a buffalo-head penny and a folded receipt; amongst it he found a crumbled dollar bill. "That should be enough." Ooh he could smell those fresh baked oatmeal cookies now. Satisfied with his bounty he patted the dandelion gently on its soft yellow head. "Good boy." The flower puffed into soft white down before bursting. Its seeds flew through the air, than it receded back to the cracks in the sidewalk.

"Hey, Hey kid!" Isaac looked up, locking eyes with a girl not much taller than himself. She had eyes painted with black shadow stretching out like an Egyptian Pharaoh. Her hair stuck up in the center like a fat Mohawk tipped in green. Shoving the contents of his despoil into the large front pocket of his hoody, he faced the blinking signal across the street. If he was going to run it had to be now. His eyes darted from the signal to the girl then back to the crosswalk; then bolted. "Hey

Wait!" Running the girl followed him across the intersection. Horns blared and tires screeched, but Isaac didn't look back. He pushed his way through a barricade of gray slacks and paisley skirts his heart racing; the cold air formed sharp crystals in his lungs with every panting breath. *Did she see?* Wisteria had told him a hundred times not to let a human catch him talking to the plants, but he hadn't counted on the girl' s arrival. Everyone else had been focused on the street lights. Losing her in the city would be difficult; he had to make it a few blocks over to Madison Park where he was certain to lose her.

"Hey kid; wait up!" Glancing over his shoulder the girl was keeping pace wearing only flip flops. She paused briefly to kick a loose stone from under foot, giving the boy just enough time to slip around the corner of *E. Mary Ave.* Isaac hoped she hadn't noticed. Darting across Main Street to the park, the soft feel of grass under his sneakers gave short lived relief. The dreaded girl was still behind him. *What on earth did she want with him*, he wondered. The tree line was only a few steps away; there he could hide from a hawk if he wanted. The girl's thongs skidded on the freshly watered grass. Her hand swung through the air in attempt to catch him, a moment later Isaac heard a thump followed by a bitten off curse word. He was safe.

Pushing herself from the ground Sam watched helplessly as boy's sneakers disappear amongst the trees. "Damn it" she cursed. She was surprised to find her foot caught in a protruding tree root. "Thanks a lot", she muttered to the tree. Jiggling her foot free of the tree root's grasp she got to her feet and dusted the dirt from her knees. A slow astounded whistle left her lips as she stare into the woods. "Well that's impressive within seconds he managed to completely vanish....hmmm". Removing the rest of the dirt from her clothes Sam headed back into the city.

Wide sea green eyes watched silently from the cover of the under growth as the girl stood up, brushed herself off and walked away. A little out of breath and a bit shaken, Isaac slid down the trunk of a basswood tree letting his head fall back to rest on its rough bark. He took a deep breath, then looked down to his holey sneakers and peeled them off. It felt good to wiggle his twelve toes, shoes just weren't made for a person with an extra toe. However, having an extra toe was useful in its own way. Eyeing a wide sturdy branch overhead he effortlessly shimmied up the tree's trunk. Once at his desired location he nestled in the crook of the branch. Fishing the booty from his pocket, he frowned. "I shall just have to go back tomorrow…" he sighed. The soft morning light and, cool breeze created a symphony that the leaves danced to. Their shadows glided gracefully across his face. Smiling he let the gentle rustle lull him to sleep.

The fire light played along her delicate cheek bones as she peered down to the bundle cradled in her arms. "Whatcha gonna call 'im?" Emerald eyes lifted from the baby, into inquisitive caramel pools staring past locks of pink and purple curls. "You know that his name is not up to me Wisteria, the child has to prove himself before Gurrell will give him a name worthy of a prince" Pushing out a lilac colored lip the girl slumped down beside the woman. "I hate my name…stupid tree". "Now, now Wisty, Wisteria is a beautiful name and don't speak so ill of him, he is our protector and provider. Gurrell is the reason this forest flourishes and without this forest we all would die." "I know.", the girl outwardly pouted. "Hey Priestess Rowan, everyone is celebrating because of this baby right? What's the big deal? A baby is born every decade around here so what's so special about him?"

Rowan's eyes drifted back down to the warm bundle in her arms. "Well Wisty he is more than just a baby. Like our protector he has a great and terrible destiny." She said with a sad soft smile on her lips. Wisteria blinked up at the Priestess in mild confusion, "What's that supposed to mean? He's just another sprite isn't he?" Rowan shook her head lightly, "To be honest Wisty I wish that were true. Within him is a mix of our kind, the wood sprites and his father's kind, the water sprites. He is special just like Gurrell was five hundred years ago."

Wisteria looked thoughtful, "oh wait... so Gurrell was a sprite too?" "Yes, and he is the reason we move and speak as we do. Sprites used to be small lights that hovered and fed off the essences of trees and animals. So long as the trees and beasts were healthy so were we. But one day a great fire threatened to destroy the entire forest and the sprites with it. Gurrell used his power to transform us into beings with arms and legs and wills of our own so we could be free. Gurrell was special, he carried with him the ability to speak with both flora and fauna where as we could only live like parasites. He begged the trees and

9

animals to take us to safety. The animals and trees opened their hearts to us and we joined with them. The water sprites road within the blood of the animals and used their legs to escape the forest. We fussed with the trees and manipulated their limbs to create our own. Over the centuries we have lost our woody appearance and knobby joints to what we are now. Gurrell chose to stay behind too weak from sharing his gift with all of us to escape. The great spirits of the forest took pity on him, sealing him inside the great sycamore; where they protected him from the fires. He remains there to this day."

The girl frowned looking down at her hands then back to Rowan. "So we were just some balls of light?" Rowan nodded. Wisteria gave the Priestess a skeptical look. "It is true" The Priestess proclaimed. "the prince will one day save us again, so it is foretold by the water sprites' sage.". Wisteria looked confused, after all what was there to be saved from? The forest had been peaceful for hundreds of years and there was no need for a savor. "But there isn't anything to be saved from."

A sad soft smile tugged once again at the woman's lips. The girl was so innocent.
Rowan then leaned down near the girl's ear. "Hey, do you want to know what I'd secretly like to call him?"

Leaning in a little closer, she whispered the name into the girl's pointed ear. "Eww, really? That's kinda dumb.", Rowan's serene face distorted into a childlike pout, "Well, what would you call him?"

Wisteria bent over hooking a finger around the soft gray moss and peered down at the sleeping infant. The girl made a face at the tufts of soft brown hair sticking straight up, and instantly knew what to call him. "I'd call him Porty after Autumn's pet porcupine." The girl stated matter of factly. Rowan shook her head and smiled, "and…you thought my name for him was silly?". "Hey what's that supposed…", her words were cut short as her face was pressed into the woman's chest. Before she could turn her head Wisty found herself being lifted from the ground and carried away. An intense heat licked her bare arms. A frightful scream bellowed from the flames slowly engulfing the village. Wisteria tried to see, but the harder she struggled to free herself, the tighter Rowan held her. "Let me go Rowan…that was my mom…let me go!" "No Wisty, the humans have come…we must Run!" Setting the girl down Rowan pulled her deeper into the forest.

The two wood sprites ran until the screams were silenced and the flames a dull amber. It was quiet from their corner of the woods. "We'll rest here."

Rowan leaned back against an ancient maple tree then gestured for the girl to do the same. "Come sit we should be safe here", but the girl didn't budge. "No! I can't believe you left them...I'm going back!" "Shh! No Wisty... if the humans catch you, you will be sold into slavery. Death would be better." Tears welled in the girl's eyes. "I HATE YOU...I HATE THAT STUPID BABY!"

"Enough, Wisty!" Rowan reached inside a satchel taking out a pinch of fine yellow powder. The tips of her fingers began to glow gold with it and she blew it into the girl's face. Wisteria sneezed then went limp. Catching the girl Rowan pulled her close. "I'm sorry Wisty we cannot allow them to find us. You don't understand how vital this baby is to our people. I cannot let the humans have him." Pressing her hands into the bark of the maple she atoned in a language only the beings of flora understood, she pleaded. "Please hide us." The roots bubbled up forming a cage made of sap and bark. Wrapping her arms around the girl and baby, Rowan ducked quickly beneath its cover.

Wisteria twitched and whimpered in her sleep. Rowan rested a hand on the girl's forehead brushing a stray curl to the side. Fighting the need to sleep, Rowan worked a piece of her own hair into a tiny bracelet. *It was a gift to her first born son the prince of the wood sprites.*

The morning came slowly. Pink and orange hues reached past the protective woody fingers to the small group huddled beneath. "Wisty…Wisty wake up I need you to get up." *Wiping the sleep from her eyes, Wisteria looked around at thick brown prison bars caging them beside the tree.* "It wasn't a nightmare was it?" *Wisty said hopefully.* "I'm afraid not…Wisty. I need you to watch over the prince for me. I'll return soon I promise…but I need to go back to the village now." *The girl's eyes lit up,* "Are you going to rescue my parents?" *Sadness welled up in the priestess's eyes,* "No Wisty…I'm afraid there is nothing I can do for your parents now." *The girl turned from the woman crossing her arms in a huff,* "Then why bother?" *Rowan took a deep breath. Placing her hands on the girl's shoulders she looked her deep in the eyes.* "Wisty I need you to be a big girl and take care of the prince while I'm gone… can you do that for me?" *Wisteria's lower lip slipped out a little then she sucked it back in.* "Fine", *she mumbled.* "Good girl." *Rowan tucked a stray purple curl behind Wisty's ear then stared down hesitantly at the boy in the girl's arms.* "I'll be back before night fall. Stay here."

As the Priestess entered the village a charred black circle greeted her eyes. The small straw and stick huts had been reduced to smoke and ash. Burnt black oily figures were scattered about in prone positions as if trying to crawl from the destruction. "I'm so sorry" a tear rolled down Rowan's cheek. Wiping the warm liquid away, she counted the remains. Two figures were locked in an embrace; although their remains barely resembled their former selves: she knew. "Jasmine, Terrance your daughter is safe. I'm sorry it's all I could do for you." Pulling some white petals from her satchel the Priestess began scattering them around singing a sorrowful chant. When she finished she set about burying the dead.

It was almost night fall when Rowan uncovered the remains of the hut that she used share with her father. Something smooth was buried in the dirt amongst the ash. Digging her worn and beaten fingers around it, she pried a small onyx box from the earth. It contained three small black beads. Thank goodness she thought. She closed the lid wiping the soot from the top. A twig snapped and she quickly shoved the small box into her pouch and turned to leave.

Stopping at the edge of the village; she bowed her head closing her eyes. In no more than a second her *eyes shot back open; her head jerking up in reflex as a sharp pain throbbed at her shoulder. "Not so fast witch."*

"MOTHER!" Isaac's outburst woke him with a start. He reached out to the nearest branch to keep from falling out of the tree. His heart was pounding. Taking a couple of deep breaths, his arrhythmia returned to normal. "Mother?"

Samantha brushed a stray hair from her face with the back of her hand and puffed out her cheeks releasing a frustrated sigh. "It's so late and I still have to make these deliveries" She turned her wrist over tapping the glass of her watch impatiently. "Shit, Marco expected me back an hour ago. If I hadn't gone back to look for that boy I would have been done already!" Strolling up the street her mind wondered back the park. She past 27th and turned up Luther Ave., before realizing that she was nowhere near the club. She stopped suddenly when she hit a rather spongy wall. Her light caramel eyes traveled up a long white shirt that was as round as it was tall. They continued up into an ugly twisted smile surrounded by wiry black hair. "Well, well looky what we have here...hey Jimmy isn't this Marco's little gopher." "I think you're right Johnny and I see she has a present for us." Jimmy and Johnny were mirror images from hell and in Sam's opinion one of their ugly mugs was enough. Samantha hugged the brown paper bag to her chest and started to back away. "Where you think you're go'n girlie" She turned to run, but her butt hit the pavement as Johnny snatched her by the collar. "Aww, look she decided to stay after all."

People passed by as she was hauled around the corner kicking and screaming. No one spared her a glance. The only witness willing to stick around was a small blue bird perched safely at the top of the building. The alley was between an old butcher shop and a massage parlor. The stench of decaying flesh accented by a musky fish smell turned her stomach; remnants of dead animal and used feminine products filled the dumpster. She swallowed hard and hugged the bag close to her body. "You can't have it fat ass go grow your own!"

"Sassy little thing isn't she Johnny" Jimmy watched as his brother tossed the girl in the back of the alley. She scooted away feeling along the slimy wet ground for something anything to help her out of this. A bottle rattled to the ground and rolled over her fingers. She snatched it by the neck and threw it straight at Jimmy's head. It missed its target, but succeeded in scaring off the bird. *Sure just leave me here* "You lil' bitch, that almost hit me. Hasn't Marco taught you any manners?" Jimmy glared at the girl then motioned for his brother to step in. Johnny cracked his knuckles "Don't worry brother I think I know how to straighten her up." Johnny's hand swung back than let it swing free like a wrecking ball. His immense paw contacted Sam's cheek and sent her flying against a chain-link fence at the back of the alley. Her head throbbed from the strike. It was followed by a sharp pain in her stomach as Jimmy drove his steel toed boot into her abdomen. She coughed. Something warm and metallic gurgled up her throat then leaked out of her mouth. Jimmy

17

crouched eye level and grinned at her swollen eye, "Not so tough now are ya girlie?" Sam choked on the rancid cigar smoke lingering on Jimmy's breath. "Go to hell!" She rolled the blood and spit around in her mouth and spat it into his face. His hand flew up and Sam winced, but instead of hitting her he wiped the spittle from his face and smeared it on her cheek. "It's a shame no one will miss a scanty little girl like you." He reached into his belt and pulled out his pistol pointing it at her forehead. She closed her eyes and did not resist. Her life sucked anyway, if this was how it would end, so be it. At least she'd never have to see Marco's face again. The hammer clicked and she waited.

Johnny steadied his brother's hand. "Hold on, she can take our message back to Marco." The hammer slowly slipped safely back into place. Sam's eyes crept open to find the two brothers talking. "What's the matter, too big of a pussy to pull the trigger?" The men looked back to the girl who was now using the graffiti-ed wall for support. "That does it!" Johnny freed the gun from his brother's hand and pulled the trigger. The bang from gun echoed off the walls. "You idiot, now the pigs are sure to show up. Come on let's get out of here!" Sam clutched her stomach feeling another sharp pain. The men's figures blurred, but she forced herself to stand. Hutched over she stood on shaky legs trying to keep the two in focus. Something stung her eyes, but she kept staring at them. "What are you looking at bitch?" Johnny pulled his arm back bringing the butt of the gun crashing down onto her temple. A flash of white pain burst behind her eyes and Jimmy and Johnny faded into darkness.

"Mother?" Isaac mulled the word over. He had never met his mother, but knew she was dead or at least the woman who gave birth to him was. He calls a different woman mother. "Hmmmm....." He shaded his eyes as the evening sun pierced through the trees. A light tap pulled his focus

from the orange rays. A small blue bird was
perched on his knee. Isaac reached out rubbing the
bird's head with his index finger then scratched it
under its chin. Pulling away the blue bird turned
and flapped as it appeared to be telling him
something of great urgency.

"What is it Sedrick?"

Isaac nodded his understanding. "Well shall we
go?"

The bird gave a little chirp and leapt up to fly in
the direction of the city. Isaac leaned back catching
the branch with his legs then flipped over to catch
another between his fingers before landing
soundlessly on the ground below. Stepping
around the tree to pick up his shoes, he followed
the bird barefoot out of the woods.

Ch. 2

"Strangers will come to our land"

Flames licked and gulped at the small stick houses. Their twisted shapes looked more like misshapen trees than homes; it gave their burning images an even more gruesome look. Screams rang through the village as arrows rained out of the darkness. Agate colored eyes watched from behind a stone shrine, as large men with hairy arms ending with sharp blades pushed through the tree line. Their arms swung like scythe harvesting the heads of all the village men. Women screamed as invaders wrenched them by the hair and ripped

21

*garments from their bodies. Children were rounded up
and placed in cages like trapped animals. Autumn
shifted her gaze through the smoke to rest on two
figures holding tight to one another near the fire pit.
Their bodies laden with arrows crashed to the ground
like fallen trees. "Mom…Dad!" Long white fingers held
tight to her narrow shoulders. "Autumn no, you can't
help them. Let's go Gurrell is waiting." Autumn's cool
agate eyes floated up meeting jewels of deep amethyst.
"But my sister is still out there!" The village elder
gently squeezed her shoulder. "Do not worry; your
sister is with the Priestess. She will be fine. Rowan
knows to meet us at the great tree… now come along."
Sorrowful eyes drifted back over the flames consuming
what was once their home, before reluctantly turning
away. "Yes Elder Sequoia."*

"Wait Autumn don't…" Wisteria groaned and
rolled over propping herself with one hand on the
trunk of an elm and pressed the other to her damp
temples. "Damn it! I could do without those
memories Autumn." She leaned over resting her
head on the coarse surface of the elm tree. "I'm
sorry Autumn I am grateful you still speak to a
blasphemer like me, even if it is only in my
dreams." Her eyes traveled past the tree's top to a

thin layer of gray smog that hovered like a malleable ceiling. "Tsk… you can't even see the stars anymore." Her gaze dropped to the mossy ground as something rattled like the chime of bamboo. A squirrel was drinking from a wooden bowl filled with a dark crimson liquid. "Get lost!" she growled. The squirrel dashed from the bowl and darted up the elm. As Wisteria picked up the bowl the remaining liquid sloshed inside. Her head was still pounding. "Rotten bilberries, I guess I have you to blame for this headache" she grumbled and struggled to sit up. The squirrel's recoil up the tree sent leaves showering to the ground. "Get off her you nasty creature!" Wisteria pitched the bowl up at the small rodent sending it leaping to another branch."…and stay off!" she shouted shaking her fist up at it. "Disgusting vermin", she complained under her labored breath. Age had taken its toll on her. It was not only difficult to move, it was also difficult to see. The forest was nothing more than tall dark figures standing out amongst the haze.

Wisteria blinked the mist of last night's indulgence from her eyes in an attempt to bring a large oak tree into slightly better focus. She stood up using the elm for support and lovingly ran her hand along its trunk before walking over to the oak. She reached out to the towering tree. It was rough, chipping, and ashy under her fingertips. She leaned down to peer into its massive hallow. "Come on now Porty, get up. It's too late to be sleeping, time for training" The wind picked up tossing some dry leaves into the fire and sent sparks popping into the air. Wisteria watched them shrivel amongst the ashes. Shivering she pulled her shawl up around her. "Damn cold…" she grumbled. *Winter will be her too soon…he's not ready.* She turned back to the hollow of the oak. It was filled with piles of clothes, blankets, tin cans, glass bottles, and various other things most people would call junk. It seemed like a day didn't go by when the boy hadn't brought something back from the city. In her opinion it all should have ended up in the trash. Wisteria reached in feeling around for the blanket; various things tumbled from its folds as she pulled it up to find the boy was gone. "Damn that boy", she cursed.

The crack of firewood called to her like a starving child. She watched the wood turn to white ash and then crumble. It wasn't going to provide much heat that way. "S'pose I should get more wood", she mumbled; then slowly moved her body along the outside of the fire being careful not to drag her skirt though its embers. It was usually the boy's job to collect the fire wood. He had been disappearing a lot lately. She had to collect wood last night as well, which is probably why she slept until the next evening. Still she was surprised by her tenacity. Wisteria had lasted longer than she could have ever expected; however, age and the aches and weaknesses that came with it did not elude her. She felt her knees give way and threw her arm out against the elm to steady herself. Taking a wheezing breath she patted the large tree. "Not to worry I won't be collecting any of your wood" Pausing to look at the boy's spot under the tree, "Why can't you stay put like a good prince?" She turned back toward the woods and hobbled away from the fire.

A.J. Zanders

Ch. 3

"Children will be taken from their homes"

Sam opened her eyes onto a dimming bulb overhead that sent eerie shadows pulsing around her; the wet asphalt beneath her hands was a blur. Her eyes rolled around in her head as she reached up to her pounding temples. She could feel blood crusting in her hair. "Ouch!" "Bastards!"

Steadying herself on the cold bumpy metal of a rusting dumpster; her stomach twisted and throbbed… it hurt to stand. Sam threw her arm around her waist, it was wet and sticky. She pulled her hand away to find it covered in blood. "How? I should be…" Her mind raced back to the

fight with the Greek brothers, the resonating
sound of Johnny's gun still rang in her ears. "He
shot me…so how am I still …alive?" She lifted her
shirt to find a scar spider-webbing from the center
just under her bra line. *Another one to add to the
collection, how wonderful.* She rested her head in a
cool palm; it felt good against the throbbing flesh.
"What happened?" Her body felt so heavy. She
leaned against the dumpster allowing the cold
metal to comfort her body. The sky was dark. It
must have been close to midnight, all the shops
were closed. People were sparse; a few ladies of
the night and an old homeless man covered in
newspapers were her only company. As she got
her bearings she noticed her stash was gone. It
would be safer to curl up in the dumpster and
wait for the morning truck to come and take her
away; than it was to go back to the club empty
handed. "Damn those bastards I wish they had
killed me…." She pushed herself off the dumpster
and made her way back to the club. A pair of
beady red eyes watched as she staggered down
the street.

Isaac came back to the park hopping through the scattered pools of light provided by the lamp post. He stopped at the edge of the forest and took in a sharp breath of cold air. Isaac dropped his head in despair. He knew full well the old bat would give him an earful for being gone so long. He looked up at the small blue bird perched on a branch above his head, "Do I have to?" The little bird puffed up and shook its tail feathers then did a little dance. Sedrick always did that when he was mocking the old sprite. Isaac laughed then nodded. "Ok let's go!" He closed his eyes and stepped into the woods allowing the darkness to swallow him completely. As if he had the forest memorized down to a single blade of grass; he hopped over fallen logs, dodged low hanging branches, and danced around shallow pools of murky water without opening his eyes once. A twig snapped under his foot and he winced. "You're late... Porty. Where have you been? Do you have any idea what time it is?" the cracked voice scolded. Isaac didn't turn around. Shrugging he waltzed over to his oak tree. Not sparing a glance in the old woman's direction; he nestled in at the base of the massive tree burrowing himself under a pile of clothing. The blue bird zipped in after him curling up under his folded arms. Despite the boy's obvious attempt to ignore the old sprite she went on. "You were out in the human city again weren't you Porty?" Isaac answered by simply saying, "Isaac." "What…what was that?" she urged holding a knobby hand to her ear. "You still prefer to be called by that stupid human name?" She shuffled over to the oak, standing over him with her bony knuckles digging into her hips as she stared at his curled form. "Are you listening to me boy?" she swung her leg back and released it right into the boy's back side. Her foot made a muffled thump as it hit all the clothing and blankets. Isaac barely budged. "I want you to stay away from there. It is nothing but trouble for both of us." Isaac rolled over looking up into her withered face and smiled, "but

I can't get oatmeal cookies out here…isn't that
right Sederick?" The little bluebird stuck his head
out from under the boy's arm and curtly nodded.
"Besides I only have one more level in *Gauntlet*
before reaching the spider queen" he said
triumphantly with a wide toothy grin. Wisty
threw up her hands, "foolish boy!" Isaac could
hear her mumbling as she walked back to her tree,
"video games….spider queen?....what a waste of
time." A victorious grin pulled at Isaac's pale lips
then he rolled over pulling the blanket up for the
night.

Across town Sam stood holding her sore body.
She stared up at the violet neon word *Enchant*. The
bright flickering purple light of the club's sign
caused her to flinch. She leaned on the double
doors of the night club and pushed. Her small
frame didn't even budge the heavy doors. About

to give up, the doors swung open. Sam would have fallen in if it wasn't for a warm solid wall. "Cat ?"

Lewie Valentino was well over six feet tall and weighed around a hundred and eighty pounds. His face was dark and heavily scared. He had thick black eyebrows that bushed above his eyes earning him the nickname 'Caterpillar' (Cat for short and only behind his back of course). The only one who ever said it to his face was Sam. Lewie's eyes widened into panic as the girl fell into his arms. "Sam! Someone call an ambulance!" he shouted. "No Cat. I'm ok really" She brushed his supporting hand aside than headed into the crowd. He watched her small battered frame get swallowed up in sweating, swaying bodies.

The room was hot and dimly lit. Colored lights swept over the crowd. A sweet smelling smoke was being fed through the vents where it hovered above their heads. People pushed together so tight you couldn't squeeze a piece of paper between them. The DJ's selection assaulted her eardrums and reverberated in her skull. She winced pressing her hands to her ears. The music was trying to split her skull wide open. The bump and grind of sweating arms and legs only served to annoy her further. She managed to manipulate her way through the choking clog of legs and arms only to get her foot stepped on. The lead footed offender had the nerve to shout at her. "Hey! Watch it you klutz!" The man seemed to realize the person he stepped on was a girl and quickly changed his tone. "Hey baby, you want to dance?" he asked pushing his crotch up against her and began rubbing up and down her thigh. Sam spun around to shove the man off her, but he quickly backed off after seeing her face. "Whoa! Chick, I don't want your problems!" The man staggered back in a drunken stupor until he bumped into two women dancing with each other. He quickly forgot all about Sam as the women threw their arms around him pulling him into their dance. Sam stared at them in disgust. "Why does Marco insist on meeting here?"

Turning on her heels she headed for the bar. Waving thick curls of smoke from her face, she approached. Her stomach churned as the smell of booze and vomit permeated her nose. The combination of sweet smoke, loud music, her injuries added to the sweaty old ash tray washed in bourbon smell was too much. She pressed her forehead against the bar's cool surface, hoping not to throw up.

"ANGELINA...ANGIE ...DO YOU THINK I COULD GET A CLUB SODA!" A woman in a waist apron and polka dotted blouse topped off with a mass of brown ringlet curls turned toward the familiar voice and smiled. "HELLO SAM SWEETHEART!" "Angie ... is Marco here?" Sam asked her face still pressed against the bar. Angelina crossed over to the counter and leaned over "WHAT DEAR... I CAN'T HEAR YOU..." she pointed up as if to indicate the speakers were right over her head "THE MUSIC..." Sam rolled her eyes, peeled herself from the counter and walked around the other side of the bar to get within ear shot of Angelina. When she was standing next to the woman under the lights of the bar Angelina gasped. "Sam honey what happened to you?" Angelina snatched Sam's shirt lifting it up for all to see and ran her hand over her stomach. "Please Angie people are staring" Angelina stepped back with tears in her eyes as she scanned Sam's face. "That bad huh?" Angelina appeared too flustered to speak. Instead she fished a rag from her apron, ran it under the facet, then set about cleaning the blood and filth from the girl's face and hair. "Angie, stop! I'm ok I just ran into the 'GEEK' brothers." Angelina dropped her rag, "OK? Sam honey, have you seen yourself? What on earth were you doing that far uptown? Those men are dangerous!" "Don't worry about it...is Marco in?" Angelina gave her a look that clearly wished the girl would go have her injuries looked at when she noticed a short bald man standing opposite the bar. She gave him a slight apprehensive nod then turned back to Sam. While Angie did not like Marco's treatment of the girl; she knew better then to cross him. "Yeah he's in the back with the rest of them. Sam honey please be careful, maybe you should just go home tonight. Marco's in a bit of a mood." Smiling Sam waved Angelina's concerns away. "When isn't he? I'll be fine really, besides he'll just be knocking on my door in the morning anyway…" Angelina shook her head, "Is there anything I can get you hon?" Sam tried to smile. "I could really use a club soda and… some pretzels would help too", the words were barely out before Sam found herself throwing her hand up over her mouth. Angelina smiled weakly and nodded, "Are you sure you won't reconsider coming back tomorrow?" Shaking her head Sam made her way to the back of the club.

Tussling bodies thinned out as she got closer to the dark hallway. A long dark corridor painted flat black, had a series of doors lining the hallway. Each door had a red light perched above its frame, and if it was on... well everyone knows what a red-light district is and this was like the mini version. The third door on the right was where Marco always met up with his clients. She reached a shaky hand out to tap lightly on the door. "Get lost", came sharply from the other side. "Marco... Marco it's me Sam." "Entrare." Gently pushing the door open, Sam peered into the dimly lit room upholstered from floor to ceiling with red velvet. A plush shag orange carpet ran along the floor and transformed into short fuzzy orange benches along the back wall. "Sammie my chicka, whatcha got for me today; was everybody happy with my product?" Sam remained behind the partially opened door. "Well girl come in." Sam reluctantly slid past the door and closed it behind her. The room was hot and stuffy due to all the vents being

closed off to prevent any smoke from getting in.
Marco sat on one of the fuzzy benches with two
women; one on either side. A side table had been
brought in just for him; it was littered with empty
water bottles. Marco leaned back tossing an arm
over each of the girls' shoulders his eyes scanning
over Sam. "Sammie you look like hell. What
happened, you smart off to one of my customers
again?!" It was as if the sight of that much blood
didn't alarm him at all. "No…I…Um ..." "Well out
with it already", his voice growing in annoyance.
"I ran into the Greek brothers..." she looked away
quickly staring at her skinned elbow "...before I
got a chance to make any deliveries." "WHAT!"
Marco stood up to his full height of five feet six
pushing his 155lb frame into her face. "Are you
telling me you lost my entire stash to those greasy
meatballs?!" "How do you think we get so many
customers to the club, eh Sammie? You want them
Greeks to get our customers?!" Sam backed away
avoiding his piercing glare, "NO. I'll make it up to
you. I just need a little time and some more
supplies. The shop upstairs is running low."
Marco drew back his smooth hand adorned from
thumb to pinkie with gold rings.

"You, stupid bitch!" Once again she felt the sting of cold metal across her face sending her to the floor. She reached up gingerly touching her stinging cheek. "You lost us customers Sammie, and customers is money. So, that means you owes me money Sammie and you have the cahones to ask me for more. I suggest you find a way to get supplies on your own" His hand drew back again and Sam steadied herself for it, but his hand stopped at a knock at the door. A deep smooth voice came from the other side. "Marco Mr. B wishes to see you" Marco turned his attention to a tall individual standing in the now open doorway. He looked back down at the girl, "You're lucky Lewie came to save you this time... but he ain't always going to be here for you Sammie." Just in case the slap didn't sink his message home, he drove his silver tipped boot square in to her stomach.

"Hey, Marco that's enough!" Marco's glassy green eyes darted toward Lewie then back to Sam. He stared coldly down at her curled on the floor then ran his manicured nails through his greasy black hair. "Well Sammie, I guess I'll just have to speak to Mr. B about this. After all, you hurt my business you hurt his, and Mr. B ain't as forgiving as me Sammie." Sam's swollen eyes opened slowly as two sets of net stockings crossed her vision as the women stepped over her body to lean on Marco. "She's just a girl Marco", one cooed in his ear; her lipstick thick on her mouth. "Yeah you can't blame her. She's just a little girl", said the other batting her false lashes against his cheek. Sam wasn't sure if they were being sympathetic or just cruel. All she could do was lay there her body too tired and sore to even move. Her eyes closed on the three and she allowed her head to be cradled by the carpet's long fuzzy orange fingers.

"Sam, are you all right?" Something warm wrapped gingerly around her waist and lifted her from the shag. She felt her body roll against the soft silk of Lewie's shirt; the smell of his cologne was woody and spicy in her nose. "Cat?" she attempted to look up at him, but he readjusted her in his arms and she could not bend her neck to see him. "Come on let's get you cleaned up"

Lewie carried her down the hall to the polished bathrooms at the back of the club. He set her down and peeled his outer shirt from his frame wrapping it around her shoulders. "Here... you can't go around like that." He gestured to her blood covered shirt. "Thanks Cat." She hugged the shirt to her sore body and headed into the bathroom. "Sam…" She stopped holding the door open with her foot. "Yeah?" Lewie gave Sam a concerned smile "When you want, I'd like for you to tell me what happened." Sam just nodded and disappeared behind the swinging door. Finally alone, the black marble and polished gold fixtures were the only witness to her tears. "Damn it!" She wiped the tears from her cheeks cursing herself. "I promised I wouldn't cry, not after father…never again." Lewie's shirt and his lingering scent calmed her, but she felt a little guilty for ruining his expensive shirt. She set it down over the sink then pulled her torn T over her head and gazed at her reflection in the mirror. The skin across her belly was covered in dry blood, but there was no bullet wound. She ran her fingers over the now fading scar. "What happened?"

Ch. 4

The ocher rays of the sun spread over the smoldering camp fire and reached through the crevasses of his cozy spot under the oak tree. They kissed his silver lashes and teased his lids. He rolled over turning his back to the persistent rays letting them warm his back. Something tugged at the tufts of his hair; he shooed at the annoyance and buried his head further under his arm. "It's too early!" The blue bird insisted; first pulling at the boy's hair then his shirt. When none of that seemed to stir him the bird burrowed under his arm and pecked him smartly in the eye. "Ow!.." Sedrick dodged the swing of arms and landed lightly on the boy's knee. Isaac pushed himself up rubbing his sore eye while glaring at the tiny bird from the other. The bird was unfazed and too busy playing with the lose strings sprouting from Isaac's tore jeans. When the bird didn't respond to his angry glare Isaac just shrugged, letting the assault go unpunished. He reached out a long slender finger and scratched the little bird under his black crested wing. "Alright I get it; I bet Mom is looking forward to some oatmeal cookies too."

The bird chirped happily and hopped up into a branch to wait. Isaac was up a few seconds later. He stopped to check on the old woman. She was snoring loudly from her usual spot under the large elm tree. Even the flowers surrounding her were curled up like wads of dark purple tissue paper. He nodded the all clear to Sedrick and was set to leave their camp. "And where do you think you are going in such a hurry?" He froze in his tracks and shifted his sea green eyes around to the hunched form that had been snoring peacefully just a moment ago. "I.."

"No, not again. You were out yesterday… today you practice." Wisteria lifted her frail body and shuffled over to where the boy stood rooted to the ground. She reached out a bony hand shoving something before his eyes. "Do you see this?..." Isaac nodded. "… And do you know what it is?" Isaac blinked at the small round object between her fingers; for a few seconds he didn't answer; then nodded again.

"An Acorn."

A mischievous grin pulled at the old woman's lips "Right, and you are not going anywhere until you can turn it into a full grown tree." She slammed the nut forcefully into his hand and turned away. "Good luck" she cackled. "Um, no thank you…all that effort always makes me sleepy." The old woman turned back around to face him. "What…I'm a little hard of hearing did you say you had a choice? Get to work." Isaac looked down at his palm where the capped nut wobbled back and forth, and sighed. "But that could take weeks!" Wisteria worked her way into a cozy spot under her tree and closed her eyes.

"Precisely, so you best hop to it." Isaac made to set the nut down quietly and leave but the woman stopped him. "And don't think of running off again...I may not look it, but I'm watching you." He looked over her relaxed form and sulked. This wasn't the first time she tried to 'train' him as she called it. Wisteria was always handing him something: a seed, a nut, a broken flower, leaves covered in mites, but each and every time he failed to do what she wanted. He would usually try and try again; eventually she would get tired of watching him. There was nothing to do but, pretend to try until she got bored.

Clamping his hands around the thick shell, he concentrated. Isaac felt his blood tingle as it ran through his veins. An iridescent juice began to flow under his skin and when he opened his palms the nut didn't have the slightest crack. "Keep working on it," Wisteria shouted. Isaac stared down at the wobbling nut in dismay. "I can't do this!" Wisteria snorted from her spot under the tree. Tossing a new log onto the fire she glared in the boy's direction from behind murky eyes. "Oh you can't... can't you I know how you've been manipulating the weeds in the city. I know you can. You just don't want to unless it benefits you."

"That isn't true," he protested "I just…it has to be a plant already for it to hear me."

"Poppycock you only say that so you can go visit that human." Isaac stared at the old hag in surprise, "what human?" A knowing glint flashed in her milky eyes. "I've seen you always waiting at the street corner for that girl to walk by." His gaze drifted away from the old woman's steely ambers. "It isn't…I don't…" "What's the matter boy? The little birdie got your tongue…ka ha ka… I knew it was about the girl. Visiting that old woman in the hospital was just a ruse." A lump had developed in the back of his throat, and as much as he wanted to deny it, he couldn't. "Can't I just do this another time?" "When? When that old bag of dust in the hospital dies or that girlie you fancy leaves town?" Isaac swallowed back his argument and settled on pleading "I promise. I'll try again when I come back." She scrutinized his visage for a moment before snorting, "Fine, but be back here before dark."…Shoving the Acorn into his pocket, his face lit up. Without another word for fear she might change her mind he spun on his heels and practically skipped toward town. As Isaac turned away, Wisteria's head fell rocking sorrowfully from side to side. "Rowan what did you do to that kid?"

The streets were quiet and the sun was just starting to warm the pavement. Isaac smiled as he made his way up Elm St and turned the corner at Mary to Aunt Lyna's Bakery. He heard the familiar chime as the heavy glass door swung open. A wave of cinnamon immediately hit his nose and he couldn't stop from salivating. Behind the counter, a woman in her mid-thirties emerged from a swinging metal door balancing a tray of scones to greet her first customer of the day. She had a soft round face that was usually splattered with some confection she had been working on that morning. Her hair was tied up neatly in a bun it was dusted with a fine mist of flour. A large white apron hugged her around the waist. It bore the evidence of a chocolate cake in the making.

"Good morning Isaac. We missed you yesterday." Isaac looked up briefly "Mornin' Lyna." Lyna was named after her great grandmother who opened the bakery sixty years ago. Isaac watched as she wiped her hands on her apron and immediately started shoving large oatmeal cookies into a white paper bag from the glass display case. His warm breath fogged the glass in anticipation. He preferred human food to the bugs and worms; Wisteria was always trying to feed him, insisting they were good…. Who wouldn't take a cookie over a mealworm? Oatmeal were his favorite, and they were becoming harder and harder for him to get his hands on, no thanks to Wisteria's persistent effort to keep him away from the city. She had become increasingly insistent about his training. He wandered why she was being so strict with him all of a sudden? His visits to the city use to be freer and now had become increasingly sparse. He peeled his eyes away from the delicious cookies and peered up at the woman behind the counter.

"So how is your Aunt Cary?" The woman paused looking down at the small boy. "Good; she's allowed to have plants in her room now." "Oh well that's good." Lyna leaned over the counter smiling. "You know Isaac she tells me you bring her a share of your cookies." She said while rolling the end of the paper bag closed. Isaac's tan completion flushed into a light pink and he looked away to fish the money from his pocket. "Um it's ok she kept me company when I needed it so…"

He wrapped his hand around the dollar bill then held it up for Lyna to take. He had to stand on his tip toes to reach the top of the counter. Lyna smiled and waved it off "These are on me this time; think of it as a thank you." She just couldn't stop her smile from widening; he was just so darn cute. She didn't know how old the boy was but Isaac had come into the bakery for the past five years, so he had to be at least ten. He must just be small for his age she thought. Lyna remembered the first time she had met him, he asked her about Cary. When she told him her Aunt Cary was receiving special care in the hospital he merely smiled and said, "Then I'll just have to go visit her".

Lyna walked around the counter handing the boy the bag. "You're a good boy." Before Isaac could utter a thank you she had wrapped her arms around him pulling him close. An underlying floral scent mingled with the stronger smells of the bakery. He felt the soft yet muscular arms that came with her job, press around him. Heat rose in his ears and he fidgeted in her embrace. "Um thank you." Lyna seemed to notice his discomfort and loosened her grip; placing her hands on his shoulders instead. She held him there a few more seconds and attempted to lock eyes with the boy, but he averted his gaze. "Well, then you take care Isaac." He was relieved when she had finally let go to open the door for him. Isaac didn't look up at her until he heard the door chime. He scooted past her quickly waving good bye.

Once outside the bakery Isaac immediately unrolled his heavy bag of cookies and reached in for his prize. He heard a high pitched chirp and looked up. Sedrick was sitting at the top of a sign post. The instant Isaac made eye contact the bird dove toward him flapping around him anxiously. "Alright, alright here" He broke off a piece of cookie, crumbled it, and held it out for his friend.

"So you talk to birds too huh?" The sound of the girl's voice made him stop and stand still as a statue. "I can still see you." Slowly his head turned toward the girl, "uh good morning?" The girl was wearing dark shades, had a stitch bandage over a split lip, and was wearing considerably baggier clothes than yesterday. His brow raised and he cocked his head to one side. Just what happened to this girl?

Sam stormed towards him her arms swinging. She was ready to run if she needed. He wasn't going to get away this time. Isaac looked her over, but did not run. Sam was now inches from his face peering into his green hoody. For a second she seemed to have forgotten what it was she was going to say. There was just something not quite right about the boy. She shook off the distraction and jabbed a bandaged finger at Isaac's chest. "Don't 'good morning me'. I got the crap beat out of me thanks to you,… you little creep. If you hadn't run off like a weirdo I wouldn't have had to chase you down, and I wouldn't have gotten lost and I wouldn't have gotten beaten up!" Isaac calmly brushed the crumbs from his hands, which were quickly gobbled up by some eagerly awaiting pigeons. When the last of the crumbs hit the ground he turned and started to walk away. Sam reached out grabbing his shoulder. "Hey, wait you little punk! I'm talking to you. You caused me a lot of trouble yesterday you know." Isaac pulled his shoulder away from her grasp, "no one made you follow me." "Listen kid, in my opinion you owe me." He stood with his back to her reaching into the paper bag. He pulled out the other half of the oatmeal cookie and shoved it into his mouth. Sam stood staring at the boy's back. "You're a real jerk you know that?!" He turned toward her giving her the biggest grin possible complete with raisins. Sam stepped back a little disgusted. "Eew gross!"

Isaac swallowed his large mouthful of cookie and with it went his sweet playful smile. "If you don't want to get hurt, then don't follow me." Sam felt her heart skip, and then it began to beat a little faster, her mouth felt dry. Suddenly she was fidgeting under his gaze. She crossed her arms in an attempt to hold herself together and averted her eyes. They settled on a tiny violet pushing its way up under a fence. Despite the desire not to push things further, she just had to ask… "you can make that grow can't you?" she said while pointing to the small purple flower. Isaac turned his back on her and started walking away. "You can can't you?" He paused for just a moment mumbling something she couldn't make out. Picking up his pace, he darted around a corner. Pigeons took to the air, blocking Sam's view in a cloud of feathers. "Hang on a second!" she yelled running after him. Her steps faltered, her body was just too sore to continue the chase. Before she knew it he had disappeared on the other side of the building; when she rounded the very same corner he was already gone. She looked left then right; there wasn't anything for him to hide under or behind. Walking over to a bench she peeked under it. She noticed a row of hedges across an empty lot were well groomed, except for one. "Humm, I wonder where he could have gone?..."

She dove at the straggly looking bush and pushed its long skinny branches aside. "...Nothing? Are you kidding me?!" She released a deep frustrated sigh baffled as to how he had gotten away this time. "Well, I'll give him credit he could be another *Houdini.*" She tossed her arms in the air gesturing that she was giving up then turned and walked away. Just to be sure she checked over her shoulder at least once, but still nothing.

When the girl was completely out of sight Isaac slipped out from under the hedges. His skin was dark and woody. *That was close.* Taking a couple of deep breaths he, let his disguise slip away. His skin paled returning to its normal light caramel color. He watched the corner suspiciously for a minute before turning back to the ragged hedge. He felt a tinge of guilt for ruining someone's hard work, but he couldn't let her confirm he could talk to plants. She would have relentlessly followed him to the hospital nagging him the entire way until he answered her questions.

The sound of air brakes hissed and Isaac pondered getting on the city bus. He knew he shouldn't. Wisteria didn't like him being in situations where people would have time to notice his unique qualities and he'd have no means of escape. But he was exhausted there was no way in his current state he could make it to the hospital let alone the park. The door swung opened and he stepped inside.

   Slowly Sam made her way back down the street
to her apartment still mulling over how she could
have lost him again in the middle of the city no
less. Her feet stopped at a set of concrete steps
leading down to a basement. It was a store room
the flower shop upstairs had abandoned when
they had gone out of business a few years ago.
They had left tools, pots, dirt and various other
supplies. Sam occupied it out of convenience. The
red wooden door to the store room sat waiting on
its rusty hinges. It should have been a cheerful
sight; her shoulders fell as she stared down at the
paint peeling from its corners. Marco had
arranged for her to work off the lost profits as one
of Mr. B's call girls. The very thought of working
for Mr. B made her queasy; her stomach had been
in knots all night. She had seen some of the creeps

that frequented Mr. B's "office". Mr. B owned the club where Marco did his "business".

The "herb" she grew was dried and burned. The smoke was pumped throughout the club. The stuff was highly addictive but virtually untraceable. It kept the regulars coming back night after night. Mr. B used the stuff on his girls as well. They happily 'worked' just to stay at the club. It was like a form of mind control. Strangely it had no effect on Sam what so ever. It was a perfect partnership Marco provided the stuff to Mr. B and Marco got a free place to hang out and sell his 'product' to the public who willingly came to him. Now that Marco was low on stash he had no money coming from sales to make up for the club's loss. Sam was being forced to make up the difference by "working" for Mr. B. If only she could get that boy to do his little trick again, he could get her out of this mess.

Sam took a deep breath trying to clear the inevitable doom from her mind. Her feet landed heavily on the concrete steps. She pulled a set of metal tools from her pocket and slipped them into the lock. Rolling the tumblers around until she heard a *click*; the door opened with a loud creak of protest. The room was small, and well lit. It had a long narrow window that faced east to catch the morning sun. It pooled over a line of plants sitting on a long table. "Hello babies how are you doing today?" Setting down her bag she turned to a skinny plant with soft blue flowers resting on a milk crate by the door. Her finger tips brushed its velvety petals. "I'll get to you in a minute sweetheart. Let me take care of the babies first ok." She crossed the room to the set of trays each sprouting with tiny leaves. They were still infants, but they were green and beautiful. Sam picked up a watering can and headed out the back door to the only working spigot down the alley.

Swinging the watering can, she hummed to herself; she had a way with plants once they started to grow that is. They wouldn't grow faster for her just fuller and more importantly a hundred times more potent. Setting the watering can down, she grabbed a handful of minerals and plunged it into the water, stirring while she hummed. "la la gro..ow for all your time...I will sing...for you ...every day ...until you are gone la la laa" She tipped the can over the plants. The water rained down over their eagerly awaiting leaves. "la la

Full and green…I shall watch…over you….la la"
Smiling as she imagined them reaching up
spreading their leaves to catch as much water as
they could.

"I knew there was a reason I kept you around
Sammie" Sam spun around dropping the watering
can. It fell with a loud metallic 'plunk', the water
splashed up hitting her bare legs and sent the rest
flowing across the floor. "Tsk tsk… you shouldn't
waist precious water like that Sammie girl; unless
you think that water will help you fill out." He
smirked eyeing her slender figure pausing at her
smooth chest. Scowling at the comment, she
picked up the can and set it back on the table. "Oh,
hi Marco. I didn't hear you come in", she gritted
through her teeth. "You shouldn't make faces like
that Sammie. How do you expect to get customers
that way?" he laughed. Marco gave the room a
quick ferret like glance, then stepped in closer to
Sam. He pressed his square stubbled chin into her
shoulder. "All joking aside how are my little pots
of gold doing today?" "They're fine. They should
be ready in a week or so." Marco lifted his chin
from her shoulder and roughly pulled her around
to face him. "Oh that isn't the answer I need to

hear Sammie. It'd be a waste having this pretty flesh tore up by one of Mr. B's clients. I suggest you make it two days or Mr. B will be having himself a new call girl." Sam glanced over her shoulder giving a pleading look at the green plants behind her and whispered "oh please grow faster." She made the mistake of looking back at Marco. His smirking face was inches from her own, "Ah, if only they would. You wouldn't be in this predicament now, would you?" Marco stepped back, running a finger along her cheek. He peered at her over the gold rim of his sunglasses. Sam avoided his piercing gaze but, was quickly forced to look at him as he snatched her chin in his hand. "Sammie... My Chicka... you will show up at the club tonight to speak with Mr. B. He is quite understanding of our problem, thanks to me. You're lucky he's willing to let you work it off, provided you come up with another supply in a few days. You should be thanking me chicka. I've saved you an entire month of hard labor." His grin widened. Sam visibly flinched, knowing all too well what he meant. Marco didn't like her reaction. "What? You don't like spending time with me!" He roughly tossed her face to the side scraping her cheek with his thumb ring. Heading for the door he paused in the middle of the room. "Oh yes, you might want someone to look at your cheek. Perhaps I'll send Lewie by later." Marco reached for the door knob, but hesitated as something light blue flickered under his nose. He stared down at the plant in disgust. "You shouldn't waste your talents on this useless thing Sammie." A wicked grin pulled at his mouth, as his hand swung free, knocking the plant to the ground. Sam watched in horror as her only treasure crashed to the ground in a pile of dirt and wood chips.

"See you at the club tonight my chicka."

Two heavy glass doors 'pinged' open. Isaac stood on a large black mat with bulky white lettering that said, St. Mary's Hospital. Lowering his head he pressed through the doors and past the reception desk. The old woman at the desk always gave him a dubious look. Once he heard her make an off comment to a coworker that young boys shouldn't wear make-up. He couldn't help the way he was born, what with his darker complexion, blue lips, silver lashes and all. It was the main reason he hid his face within the oversized green hoody. Keeping his head down and clutching a bouquet of flowers in front of his face, he made his way to the elevators. The elevator doors slid open with a soft 'ping'. Excused himself, he slipped past a couple exiting and nestled in a back corner after pushing the glowing 6 on the panel. The elevator stopped on the third floor allowing a janitor with a cleaning cart on. His thick lidded eye's punctuated with dark circles slid towards Isaac and he forced a smile. He looked as if the effort used up the last of his strength. "Nice flowers. They are sure to make someone happy." Isaac held the flowers higher, hiding the blush warming his face. Mercifully, the elevator stopped on the sixth floor and Isaac stepped off. He waved to the man who shared the short journey with him. Turning on his heels, his sneakers squeaked as he strolled along the white linoleum hall.

He hugged the paper bag and flowers to his chest, and reached out tapping lightly on the thick metal door. A frail voice barely drifted through the steel, "Come in." Isaac pushed the door open. His eyes closed in protest at the light shining through the room's only window. Forcing his silver lashes open, they focused on a frail woman struggling to sit up in her hospital bed. "Hello Mother." Cary's thin lips turned up into a warm and welcoming smile. "Good morning Isaac…I missed you yesterday. Are you doing all right?" His eyes traveled pensively over her stationary form; it had been five long years and she was still here. Isaac knew about many plants that aided in healing, but nothing could cure what Cary was suffering from. He hated feeling so useless. "I'm fine" he finally said in a soft whisper. Placing the flowers beside her bed, he pulled a chair up next to her. "What about you? How are you doing?" Little wrinkles bracketed her eyes as she smiled. "Don't worry about an old woman Isaac… just take care of yourself." Her vision drifted toward the flowers Isaac had set by her bedside. "Lilies, you know I love lilies. Oh but it's too early for them to be open." A look of sadness crossed her features. Isaac lifted them from the table. Lowering his face among the flowers, he whispered, "Bloom" As he lifted his head, the flowers burst open in pink and orange glory. Cary gasped with delight. She had seen him do similar things before, but it never failed to amaze her; however she knew. Keeping his talent a secret was an uncompromising rule Wisteria set upon him for going into town. "Isaac! You shouldn't do that here. What if someone sees you?" Pouting, his eyes darted away from her, "sorry...I just wanted..." "It's okay hon. Come here", Cary patted the bed next to her and Isaac gratefully hopped in beside her. "Isaac, do you remember when we met?" she asked hugging close. Isaac nodded. "You looked so lost yet so sure of yourself... even for one so small."

The winter snow was all but a memory; only small white patches remained under the shadow of the trees and benches. The rest of the park was green with grass that was dotted with dainty yellow and purple flowers. Trees were sporting the first buds of spring. Cary sat at one of the benches clutching a white paper bag in her hands. The bag had pink letters scrawled across it that read, "Aunt Lyna's Bakery".

  The warming air felt good. Winter had been long, and the sun's warmth was welcome. Looking around she waited patiently for her usual visitors. She didn't have to wait long. As soon as she unrolled the paper bag, birds flew in from every direction. "Hello little ones, do you want to share some of my oatmeal cookies?" Crumbling up the cookies, she tossed the crumbs among the hungry pigeons. Occasionally a squirrel would dart in scattering the birds temporarily, as it snatched a bigger piece of cookie to eat in the safety of their tree, prize proudly in paw. That day, the pigeons scattered, but the credit didn't go to a squirrel. When the birds had flown off to rest in the branches and on the tops of lamp posts; Cary found herself staring at a small boy. He was dressed in a worn and stained multi-colored sweater that was several sizes too big. Curious aqua colored eyes fringed with thick silver lashes stared at her. Long spiky hair topped a small pixie face. His lips were a light shade of blue. "Poor thing he must be freezing", she thought. "Hello" she greeted. The boy stood still and continued to stare at her. His eyes lowered and fixated on the white paper bag in her hands. "Would you like a cookie?" The boy cocked his head to one side he appeared to be playing with the

63

word 'cookie' "Cookie?...what's a cookie?" Cary could not help but laugh. "You don't know what a cookie is love?" She quickly regretted laughing for the boy now seemed hurt. "I'm sorry...Here..." She reached into the bag and pulled out a fat oatmeal cookie. She held it out to him. He stepped an inch or so closer, just outside the reach of her fingertips. Snatching the cookie he took it up into the nearest tree. He reminded Cary of a squirrel. "Wow!" She set her bag down and walked under the tree the boy had climbed. "You don't have to be scared you know..." The boy didn't show any signs of relaxing, as he quickly stuffed every morsel of cookie into his mouth. He looked around the tree top, then down to the woman standing below. "Ah um...you did that so well...I've never seen anyone climb a tree so fast!" He watched as she fished inside her purse for something. "Want to try something else really good?" Cary asked as she continued to dig in her handbag. She found what she sought after and held it up for him to see. He flinched as she waved it up at him, but when he realized it wouldn't bite, it was a very curious object. The small round thing was enclosed in a bright colored wrapping of some sort.

The boy seemed hesitant, she acted on instinct. Unwrapping the small object she popped it into her mouth. "Mmm see it's yummy." Pulling another one just like the first from her purse, she held it up to him. The boy scooted down, leaned back catching a branch between his legs and snatched the small object from her hand. Before she could blink, he had pulled himself back up in two quick movements. Sitting perched on a branch, he began mimicking her earlier gesture. He removed the wrapper from the small object then popped it into his mouth. It was soft, and sweet, and had a flavor he wasn't familiar with. It kind of tasted like the cookie, but different. He liked it. Satisfied Cary watched the boy enjoy his candy. She quietly returned to her bench. Glancing over her shoulder, she felt the boy behind her. Looking around; she felt a tinge of disappointment when she didn't see him. A large shadow flicked across her field of vision causing her to look up. The boy was hopping from tree to tree following her as she made her way back to the bench.

Sitting back down, she heard a light thump as the boy landed under a tree just a few steps from her. He seemed conflicted; should he approach her, or stay where he was? "It really is a beautiful day to share with someone", she said to no one in particular. She pretended not to see the boy as he hid behind the tree. Before she knew what was happening, the boy had seated himself right next to her. "Well hello", she said acting surprised to see him there. "Can I have another cookie?" he asked hopefully. Cary frowned, "I'm sorry I don't have anymore." The boy looked devastated and made a quick move to leave. "Wait! Please if you promise to meet me here again tomorrow... I promise to bring you more." The boy nodded, settling back down on the bench. They sat in awkward silence for some time. The sun started to set and the park lamps flickered to life. "I guess I should be getting home...it was lovely to have met you...er" "....Well I never got your name sweetheart" The boy looked away a bit embarrassed. "Why, what is the matter? It can't be that bad I won't laugh I promise." The boy looked down at his hands the candy's crinkled wrapper still clutched in his fingers. "I don't really have a name...my Aunt calls me 'Porty'. It was the nick name she gave me when I was a baby, but I don't actually have a name." For a moment Cary was speechless. "Well is it ok for me to call you Porty? I don't know what else to call you." The boy violently shook his head 'no'. "I don't really like that name." Her thin fingers flew up to her lips as if she had just said something offensive "Oh I see. I'm sorry. What would you like for me to call you?"

The boy shrugged staring at the crumbled wrapper in his hands. Cary sat deep in thought until a small voice startled her. "I have a secret name, my mom gave me." "Your mom?" Cary asked in surprise. "Well I think she *is my mom. I see her in my dreams sometime. I like the name she gave me, but my Aunt says it's a stupid name for a sprite." The word 'sprite' threw Cary off for a moment, but she chalked it up to childhood nonsense. Leaning down, she looked the boy in the face. "I can keep a secret. So could I call by your secret name?" A toothy grin spread wide across his face; he nodded, then leaned over and whispered it in her ear.*

Cary's cheeks burned with embarrassment. She felt a little ashamed by the memory. After all she had treated him like a wild squirrel back then. It wasn't until a few years later that she realized the word 'sprite' had significance. There was no way he was a human. Cary had met him nearly thirty years ago yet, he was still so young; unfortunately, she had aged like the human she was. Her lips sagged into a frown as she looked at her spotted hands. Isaac still looked as young and child-like as he did the day they met. Goodness he was still wearing the green sweatshirt she gave him years ago, even though it was faded and torn in places. "Isaac, why don't you let me make you something other than that worn-out green hoody you always wear?" He shook his head, "this is the first thing you gave me." Cary blushed, "I'm sorry, I bought you one so large. I thought you'd have grown into it by now." Isaac shook his head again and smiled, "I like it." Cary reached and touched the boy's cheek, "I'm glad", she whispered. It was if that simple act zapped the last of her strength. Her hand dropped to the bedside. "I'm sorry Isaac. I get so tired lately." His smile faded and concern filled his eyes, "Mother, are you ok?" Cary responded with a weak smile, taking a ragged breath before pushing herself up. "That's enough about me...I have something for you. It's in the drawer of my nightstand." She gestured to the side opposite of where Isaac sat. He stood and walked over to the nightstand. Opening the drawer he found a jar with holes punched in the lid. He held it up to the light and smiled. "A horned beetle!" he cried. Looking at the woman he noted that her features had softened, "it crawled up my night gown when I was out in the garden yesterday. I had to hide it so the orderly wouldn't take it." She laughed lightly at the thought. "The little bugger kept crawling where it didn't belong". Her eyes drifted closed. Her breathing slowed. "Mom...?" Cary didn't respond. Her chest rose and fell in shallow breaths until stopping all together. Machines started beeping frantically, "MOM...!"

The metal door swung open and three nurses rushed in shoving him aside. They unceremoniously ushered him out the door without a word. Isaac's sea green eyes clouded as women in white surrounded Cary each one holding metal instruments or pushing boxes with wires sticking out from them. The door closed shutting him out from the chaos inside. Fear gripped his stomach "Mom?!"

A.J. Zanders

Ch. 5

"Our men will be slaughtered"

The dark oak door loomed in front of her like something ominous. She lifted her hand and then let it fall. Taking a deep breath she tried again. Before she could touch knuckle to wood, a deep order reverberated through the door. "Come in child!" Her shoulders slumped as she lowered her arm to turn the handle slowly opening the door. The room held an odd assortment of items. A large wooden desk sat in its center, with two dark velvet chairs resting in front. Strange animal prints adorned the walls. Behind the mahogany desk sat a very large man in a light purple pinstriped suit. His dark lips pulled back into a shark-like smile. "I'm so glad you decided to come Samantha...Marco has told me you lost his stash the other night and it looks like you are in charge of paying off his debt. Ordinarily I would give you a choice to work it off in a few nights, or to work here at the club for a few weeks until it is paid off, however..." his bulbous eyes traveled over her thin legs and across her narrow shoulders. "...I believe due to the circumstances, you'd best pay them off quickly. Believe me, I am normally a patient man, but I can't let your little slip up mess with my business." Sam fidgeted under his roaming eyes wishing she owned something other than a pair of cut off shorts and a few ratty T-shirts. She released a tense breath when he finally dropped his gaze. He reached for a stack of cards sitting on his desk in a gold holder shaped like praying hands. The purple business cards had the insignia of the club scrolled across it in gold lettering. He slipped one from between the fingers of the holder, "I want you to take this..." he said sliding the card across the desk toward Sam. "I run a rather respectable escort service here, so get yourself something nice to wear for my client. He rather likes them young...but he'd prefer they have a little class." He glared at her attire once more then his bulbous eyes traveled to the top of her dyed green hair and his lip curled as if smelling something putrid, "You might want to borrow a wig from downstairs." His mouth twitched in a malicious grin, "...relax child. If he likes you, your debt could be paid off in a day or two. That should give you enough time to re-supply my club. Am I right?" Sam nodded hesitantly, reaching out; she plucked the card from the desk to examine it. "That is a special card I keep for uptown shops. I am a very good customer. They will know what to set you up in." His smile widened. "You're dismissed...oh, and child...be here at seven sharp tomorrow night. My client does not like to wait!" He lifted a meaty paw and waved her out. Sam lumbered out of the room still holding the card. Flipping it back and forth she wondered, "What am I supposed to do with this?"

Looking down at her normal attire she sighed, "I guess this isn't good enough for a call

girl." Her sarcasm did nothing to deal with her
bubbling nerves.

Isaac held the jar, with the black beetle, up to the
lamp light. Something this good usually made him
happy, but now….. "What's wrong with you
Porty? I told you to be back here before dark."
Isaac quickly hid the jar behind his back as the old
woman entered the halo of light. His actions
caused a thin gray line to rise up into her
peppered curls. "Whatcha got there Porty?" she
asked suspicion coating her voice. "Nothing." He
proclaimed as he backed up keeping the jar away
from her roaming gaze for as long as possible. "If
it is nothing, then let me see it. It's from that
retched girl isn't it?" "No…it's really nothing." He
shook his head violently keeping the beetle out of
her sight. "Enough of this" Wisty reached into her
pouch and pulled out a fine golden powder.

Before Isaac realized what was going on she had blown the golden cloud right into his face. His eyes widened and his body stiffened. In the time it took for Wisteria to dust the powder from her hands, he had fallen to the ground like a dead tree. The jar landed behind him. "Ha, so this is what you were hiding eh, a present from your human?" She rattled the jar causing the beetle to tip over on to its back. Its legs were swimming wildly through the air. "Maybe I should keep this for myself as payment for you being late. You'd just waste it anyway. Bugs are meant to be savored, not kept as pets." She worked her knobby hands at the lid, but it proved too tight for her. "Hmm, I could just bust this thing open." Her arm went up holding the jar high, as she got ready to smash it against a rock. Hearing a loud sneeze she turned toward the boy, struggling to stand. "Ah, you are recovering all ready, quick even for a sprite." Isaac tried to protest, but his tongue felt like lead. He moved his lips but no words came. His face twisted in annoyance as the old sprite laughed at his struggles. Finally, he found his voice again. "No! Please …it may be the last thing I have from Mom." Wisty peered at the jar, than slid her gaze over to the boy. Shaking the jar at him she stated, "You know that old hag isn't your real mother." Isaac fell against the tree and ended up landing in the dirt. His head throbbed between his fingers. Wisteria laughed, "Ka...you shouldn't get up so fast after such a dose."

Isaac continued to rub his temples while he mumbled, "don't call her an old hag! It doesn't matter that she isn't my real mother...I care about her." Wisty's face fell, and she tossed the jar back at the boy. "I am too soft with you.... No excuses tomorrow you practice all day. You got that!?" she emphases her pronouncement by point her long, yellow jagged nail at his chest. He nodded. Wisteria seemed satisfied. "Good. Now...go get some firewood so we don't freeze tonight. Remember only gather the ones that are already on the ground!"

When Isaac returned with the firewood the old woman was snoring. A line of drool ran down the creases of her mouth. He shook his head and set about piling the sticks and leaves needed for kindling. He softly padded over to the old woman and reached behind her for the flints she kept under the Elm.

He felt the two jagged rocks between his fingers. As he drew them out, he was grabbed by something callused and bony that grinded into his wrist. "Stop! You must never use these, Porty." Isaac blinked down into stern ambers eyes. A look of shock and confusion played across his features. Wisty snatched the rocks from him. Her body creaked and cracked as she pushed herself up and over to the fire pit. She squatted near the circle of rocks and began banging the flint stones together. The dry leaves sizzled and popped as the thin twigs slowly began to burn. She blew lightly on the glowing tinder until the large logs burst into orange flames. "I could have done that you know." His voice weak in protest "Never!" she screamed.

Cautiously Isaac backed away. He had never seen that look in her eyes before. It wasn't anger… it was more like sadness, bordering on fear. He made his way over to the fallen trunk beside the fire and stared with curiosity at the old woman as she poked the burning wood.

Once the fire was burning steady and the woman had settled against her tree, Isaac ventured to ask, "Well, it seems like so much

trouble for you; if you would just let me…"
"Never! You understand!" She threw one of the
flint pieces at him. "…What good was all of this if
you do that?" The stone hit his forehead with a
thumb before tumbling to the ground. Isaac
touched his skin where the rock had made contact,
"I'm sorry…I didn't…" He pulled a dab of purple
sap-like liquid from his wound and stared at his
fingertips. Wisteria took a deep breath and
stomped over to him. Grabbing his wrist she
whipped his hand to the side willing his gaze to
meet hers. "Listen to me!" His sea green eyes
remained down cast, even though the dull ambers
of the old woman were boring a hole into his
skull. Releasing a heavy sigh, she dug into her
pouch for a small jar. She pulled the jar's stopper
and dipped a finger into the thick yellow gel
before dapping it onto his forehead. "We
sacrificed everything to keep you alive. What
good are you to any of us without your powers?!"
Isaac blinked up at her in bewilderment
"Powers?" His sorrowful eyes stared into angry
pools of molten amber.

 Pulling a fuzzy leaf from a nearby shrub,
Wisteria pressed it to his forehead with her

thumb. "You have a gift Porty that only you possess and without them you won't be able to save the forest."

"What do you mean, without them...I can't really do anything with them!" he pouted. "Shut up Porty! Don't talk about things you don't understand", she said pressing the leaf a little harder into the cut. He winced, but the bleeding had stopped. Now if only the throbbing would cease. Wisty shook her head mumbling under her breath. "I guess it is time..." Her tired eyes drifted away from the boy and into the darker shadows of the forest. "Maybe I should face my own demons as well" Turning from the black abyss, she smiled like some mad scientist at the boy, who was still poking the sore spot on his brow. "But we have much to work on before then..." His hand fell and a sudden unease settled into the pit of his stomach.

A.J. Zanders

Ch. 6

"Again!" she commanded "I can't, it isn't working!" he whined in protest. "Do it again!" Isaac stared down into his cupped hands and concentrated; he felt his fingers heat up as he pushed more energy into his palms like Wisteria had taught him. The harder he concentrated, the harder he squeezed his hands around the shell. Suddenly it cracked, cutting his palm. He opened his hands examining the injury. Where a piece of the shell had broken loose, a thin tentacle was wiggling out. "Wisty look!" He held the seed out for her to see. It wobbled and the broken seed burst open as the sprout pushed its way between his fingers. "Don't get too excited…" she said pointing to the seedling in his hands "that… is not a tree!" Despite the old woman's criticism, he felt rather proud of himself. A self-satisfied smile crept over his lips. The excitement of his accomplishment went buzzing though his head. He felt giddy and light headed; suddenly, the old woman and forest faded into a haze. The last thing he saw was the ratty stitching of the old sprite's wool skirt.

Outside the dressing room, Sam stood in front of the department store mirror. Her face fell in disgust. "I can't wear this!" "Why not? I think it looks good on you." Sam spun around to glare at Lewie Valentino, who was casually leaning against a pillar. "Cat, what are you doing here?!" He pushed himself off the pillar and strolled over for a better look. His brown eyes traveled from the tailored jacket down to her narrow hips draped in a matching pair of pants. "Very nice...maybe you should apply at the offices in town after you finish with your date." Sam's face scrutinized his countenance for any hint that he was serious. "I'm kidding!" Turning her back to him, she looked back into the mirror. "I know I look stupid." "I didn't say that Sam. Listen..." he stepped up placing his hands on her shoulders and spoke to her reflection in the mirror. "...if you don't want to do this, you don't have to. I could pay Mr. B for you. I don't mind. Really...it is the least I can do." Holding up her hand she stopped his babbling, "Cat...you need that money for your mom's hospital bills right. I'm a big girl I can handle this." Lewie Closed his eyes and took a deep breath before opening them and meeting her gaze, "but Sam it was my fault the Greek brothers took your stash." Sam whipped around pushing his hands off her shoulders. "What!"

Lewie lowered his arms and slumped into a nearby chair. "I was supposed to meet with them that evening to give them their usual stash, but something came up and I couldn't make it." Sam met his eyes with a fierce gaze "Why on earth are you giving the Geek brothers our stash? Do you have any idea how long it takes me to grow that shit?!" Her fists were clenched so tightly that her knuckles were white. She wanted to scream at him, but she just couldn't manage the words. Heat ran from her toes all the way up to her ears.

Sam stormed back into the dressing room to try another outfit on. "It isn't what you think…listen…I just wanted to protect you" he called after her. Sam stomped back out a few minutes later wearing a long glittering pink gown. It had spaghetti straps and cut low in the front and back, but it pooled around her feet.
"How on earth does that protect me?!"

Lewie blinked at her angry face. It was almost as pink as her dress and as a result, he just couldn't take her seriously. He laughed. What was he supposed to do she looked like a little girl trying on her mother's clothes then pouting because she couldn't wear them outside. Her attitude was only helping the image. "Pu..ff ffee…Please try something else on", he chuckled while waving her back towards the dressing room. Her face turned an even darker shade of pink. Did she really look that foolish?

"Fine!" Turning in a huff, she stormed back to the dressing rooms; one fist, swinging at her side, while the other held up the dress so she wouldn't trip on it. Her little tantrum only helped set the image of a pouting child into Lewie's mind. His laughing was cut short; however, by the sight of her bare back covered in long scars. He knew all too well where she had gotten them. It had only been a few years since Sam had come to the city; before that she had lived on a farm several miles out with an Amish family. She was beaten almost daily and forced to use her skills with the plants in the fields. She was molested by her 'brothers' almost every night, and was locked up in the cellar with only a straw mat to sleep on. Her life had never been easy, but she was strong. When she told Lewie about living on the farm she didn't even shed a tear. Lewie stood up and shook the dismal memory from his mind. Walking over to the entrance of the dressing room he said, "Sam I'm sorry I didn't mean to laugh." "Oh you seemed to be having a good time to me!" she retorted. Lewie tossed his hands up in defense, "Seriously, I'm sorry."

"Whatever. ….You still haven't explained how giving our stash away to the 'Geek' brothers helps me. … Does Marco know you did this?" Lewie lowered his head and stared down at his polished leather shoes. "No…"

The door to the dressing room swung open. Sam stood in the open doorway wearing a pair of tight black Capri pants with a sea blue sleeveless silk top gathered in the middle with a gold belt. Lewie felt his jaw slacken, "ahh…" Sam glared at him. "What… are you going to tell me this looks stupid too?" Lewie shook his head unable to tell her what was really going through his mind. Sam strolled past him and stepped in front of the mirror. A slight smile tugged at the corner of her lips. "Better…", she told herself, then spun back around facing her critic. "Cat are you going to tell me why or not?!"

Lewie shook the shock from his features and allowed her question to sink in, then he walked over placing his hands gently on her shoulders and smiled, "don't worry about it ok? I swear it won't happen again." he kissed her tenderly on the forehead and turned to leave the store. "I'll keep an eye on you from now on… I promise." He waved goodbye leaving Sam standing there touching the warm spot left on her forehead by his lips. She felt the heat rise in her cheeks as she stared after him; unable to wave, or even say goodbye. "You look very nice miss." Sam twisted around to glare at a bubbly sales girl in a faux fur vest, black mini, and knee high boots. The girl fluttered her false lashes at Sam. "Is he your boyfriend?…What a cutie. Can I help you find some sexy sandals to go along with that glamorous look?" No, it wasn't like that; yeah he was a 'cutie'; and no she didn't want this annoying girl's help. She didn't even want to be here. She wanted to tell the girl to get lost. That she was getting dolled up for some perverted businessman and why didn't the sales girl mind her own bee's wax? Sam said none of those things. She nodded instead and found herself saying, "if you would please."

The room had a hazy red halo drifting in the air above the booth. The Greek brothers, Jimmy and Johnny, were meeting with two guys they would hardly call friends. Mr. B had requested an audience with the brothers. He seemed desperate. The southern gentlemen leaned back dabbing sweat from his brow and waving the smoke away from Jimmy's cigar. The other man sat in the shadows and never introduced himself. "Y'all listen here, it's not that business hasn't been good since that little Sicilian shrimp came into my club. I just don't need the trouble he brings with him", he drawled in a heavy southern accent as he stirred his mint julep with a thin pink straw. The large southerner continued, "I've had to pay off the police twice this month. If I paid you half of the hush money I've had to pay the police, for your stash; you'd still make it out like fat hogs!"

Johnny whistled, "Woo… that's a lot of dough those pigs have been collecting lately. I wouldn't mind getting in on some of that." Jimmy puffed on his cigar, blowing a thick cloud across the table. "So you want us to take over the market and keep the police out of your club?" Johnny reached across the table to grab the bowl of peanuts then leaned back dropping a handful of the salty nuts into his mouth. The fat southerner raised the thin pink straw to his chubby dry lips and smiled. "Can I make a suggestion? You're going to need the girl. I've been keeping her busy at the club what with the money she owes me. I'm sure she hasn't had the time to grow him anymore, but she is a stubborn one. Although small, Marco came up with a new stash just this morn…" Before the man could finish speaking Johnny had sprayed a mouth full of nut pieces into the man's face. "Vat wittle bitch is still ovif?!" (that little bitch is still alive?) The man's dark brow shot up at Johnny's outburst. Jimmy tossed a hand up stopping his brother, "I apologize for my brother's rudeness." "So Mr. B, would you have us kidnap the girl and risk pissing off the police who have been greasing their palms with money from your club? What

89

exactly is in it for us?" Mr. B sputtered mint julep, as his bulbous eyes bulged. "You would turn down such a generous offer, and then, have the nerve to insult me!" The dark figure that had remained silent stood up and said, "You'd have a corner on the market of the most potent and addictive drugs available. The girl hates Marco. She is the only person capable of growing the plants in the middle of the city." The man stepped out of the corner and into the dim lights. They cast eerie shadows down his nose and across his thick bushy eyebrows. "Ah have you turned Benedict Arnold on your old pal Marco…Lewie Valentino?"

Ch. 7

"Our land will be stolen"

{"It looks to be another dry day tomorrow." "I sure wouldn't want to have stock in peaches this year." "Peaches Jerry? Well, I don't know about you, but I'd miss my grandma's peach pies" "Whatever Jerry…Well you heard it folks, so drink lots of water and don't get your hopes up on any peach pies"}

Sam threw her arms behind her head sighing as the two men argued on the radio. The florescent bulb above her cot twitched its last few moments of life. It had been two days since she had seen the mysterious boy whom she lost in the park and again at the bus stop. Her eyes traveled over to the outfit hanging on the door, and sighed. "Why do I have to repay his debt? That bastard!" Her light brown eyes drifted from the outfit to the withering plant resting on the milk crate. The stem was bent in half, and the deep green leaves had become a patchy yellow. One of its light blue petals broke free and floated to the ground. "No…no no no!" She pushed herself up, and swung her legs around to the bed's side. Standing she hurried over to the dying plant. "No, don't die on me. Come on you're all I have left. Please…" She scooped up the pot and ran outside to the spigot. Holding it under the water for a few minutes, she sang to it softly, "it's ok little one…mmm… I will always be here for you….mmm… I'll give you my strength so you can grow big and strong…mmm." Another petal broke free and drifted down landing on her bare foot. "Seriously, you have never left me before

….all you ever needed was for me to sing to you and you'd perk right up!" A third petal snapped free and landed on her arm; her heart sank and her body caved. She slumped down in the alley fighting back tears. Her throat tightened when the face of a certain boy entered her mind and her heart skipped for just a second; he could help her she knew he could. She had seen what he had done with that dandelion, but would he help? Running back inside, she set the plant down. Sam ran out the front door and up the street.

"Porty!...Oi Porty wake up it's morning!" Isaac woke when he felt something thumping him in the leg. "What…?" his vision was fuzzy as he struggled to see her. "For pollen's sake, you could sleep through a buffalo fart." His sea green eyes looked up into the wrinkled face staring down at him in concern. "What happened?" he asked rubbing his eyes. He heard her mumble something as she walked back to her spot under the elm. "Porty, you passed out, and you've been out since yesterday." He blinked a few times pushing himself up. Something soft and fuzzy moved in the palm of his left hand. His fingers uncurled to reveal the nut had completely shattered around the roots of a tiny plant. "I did it?!" "Don't get so excited we don't need you passing out again." Lingering behind her jest was a hint of praise. Although Isaac wasn't paying attention, he kept staring at the tiny walnut growing from his will alone. "Wait what is it….?"

Upon closer inspection he noticed the sprout's pulse echoed in his own; the roots had burrowed deep into his skin. Tiny hairy tentacles were swimming through his veins. "Ahh..!" Isaac quickly ripped the plant from his palm and tossed it to the ground. "Ka ha ha… got a little attached to you did it?" He tore his shocked gaze from the plant on the ground, to the old woman cackling to herself. "Why would it do that?" "Because you were asleep and didn't plant it into the ground it took its nourishment from you. Be careful now your blood is like super-charged deer shit to a plant." Isaac stared down at the tiny holes left in his hand by the roots of the walnut.

The old woman downed some liquid from a small wooden bowl then gazed absently at her reflection in the burgundy pool. "Don't worry that won't always happen. You were just so set on getting it to grow you offered yourself to it…just be more careful in the future." Isaac continued to stare at his hand then the tiny walnut. He shook the image of the plant burrowing into his veins out of his mind, and then reached out to dig a hole in the dirt, placing the plant deep in the soil. "Feel sorry for it do ya?" Isaac's face fell, "That wasn't its fault." Wisteria yawned "Maybe you aren't such a waste after all", she said sleepily. "You'll need to get some water for it now…" her voice trailed off and she allowed the warm sun to gently lull her to sleep. "Wisty…I…" Isaac lifted his head hearing a faint *thump* as the bowl rolled away from Wisty's limp hand. "Hmm?" Picking up a blanket, he laid it across the old woman's shoulders and headed toward the park, bowl in hand.

The grass was wet from the sprinklers. It was cool between her toes as she walked barefoot over the freshly cut lawn of Madison Park. As she got closer to the tree line, Sam shouted for the boy who got away. "Hello...Hello...are you here?...I brought you some cookies!" She held a white paper bag up high. *Lyna's Bakery* was printed on the front in pink lettering. Waving it back and forth, she hoped the boy would see her. "Come on, I just want to talk." She let her arm fall to her side, tapping the bag impatiently against her bare leg, as she looked around the park for any sign of the boy. "Heeellooo…", she knew he was here, but where? She combed her thin fingers through her coarse hair and sighed. "Hey if you're listening, I just wanted to say I was sorry about the other da..." A rustling sound came from a bush behind her; she spun around with mild anticipation. A small reddish brown rodent with a fluffy tail scurried across the grass and up the nearest tree. "Stupid squirrel." She looked around once more pulling her jacket around her. Her shoulders fell in disappointment. "He has to be here", she thought. "Come on, if you bring a guy cookies…he should at least come out and get them." Sam scanned the park once more; a picnic table sitting out in the open caught her eye. "Well that could work." Waltzing out into the clearing, taking large deliberate steps over to the table she would set her "trap". She set the bag down in the middle of the table looking about for any and all vantage points while backing away. "Ok, I'll just leave these here then…."

Keeping a close eye on the bag, she made her way over to a trash can sitting next to a large tree. She ducked behind it feeling confident about the hiding spot, thanks to the tree covering her back. The table was in clear view. "He has to step out into the open", she said to herself. "There is no way he can sneak away with them."

"Sneak away with what?"

Sam turned around coming nose to forehead with the very boy she was looking for. "AAhhhh!" Her arms went wind-milling through the air as she tried to regain her balance managing to tip the trash can over. The contents started pouring into her lap causing her to fall over backwards in her attempt to escape. Her antics sent the can rolling across the park! Isaac hung upside down a minute longer giggling to himself, before flipping over and landing at the tree's base. Sam was mortified. All she could do was sit there staring at the boy's back as he strolled past her into the field, snatching the bag off the table. Isaac waltzed back over to her and crouched in front of her sprawled form. The paper bag swayed between his knees and a huge grin plastered his face. "Whatcha doing?" Sure rub salt into my wounds already thought Sam. What was with this kid? The first time she tried talking to him he had practically bitten her head off. *Great, I need help from a psycho* she thought. She wanted to scream at him, hit him then beg him for his help, but her mouth just opened... then closed.

Isaac shrugged and stood up to walk away, "Okay... well thanks for the cookies lady." Bewildered, she sat there a minute longer. Who did he think he was fooling? She couldn't forget the chill she got from the look in his eyes just a

few days ago, when he told her *not to follow him.*
"Cut the crap!" Her words sliced through his
carefree demeanor he stopped in his tracks.
Turning around his impish smile faded, and was
replaced with one that was too old and sad. Sam's
stomach twitched as if containing a swarm of
angry wasp. She quickly averted her gaze. "I'm
sorry…."

   Shrugging off the girl's outburst, he turned to
walk away "I have to go now." "Hey wait! I know
we got off on the wrong foot…um…well my
name's Sam what's yours?" Isaac looked over his
shoulder to her outstretched hand then, into her
pleading caramel eyes. "Isaac", he answered
rather succinctly. He turned away ignoring her
hand and opened the white paper bag, "Hey this
isn't cookies." It was Sam's turn to give the little
imp a devilish smile of her own. "No…" She held
up an identical white paper bag, "… but these are,
and you can have them if you can fix it" she
gestured to the bag in his hand. Isaac reached in
and pulled out a small lanky plant. Carefully he
examined her face looking past the yellowish
leaves. "What does this plant have to do with
cookies?" he asked nodding toward the other bag.

"You can fix it… can't you? I've seen you. Normally I would just sing to it, but I think it is too far gone now… so I thought…" The boy pouted. "But…I can't" Sam's face twisted into disappointment, followed by disbelief. He was her last hope it took all of her strength not to throw the cookies at him. "Come on, I saw you do something with that dandelion. I know you can fix it." Isaac avoided her hopeful gaze, and stared down at the sickly plant in his hands. "I've never fixed a dying plant before. I…can barely communicate with ones that are doing fine on their own." Fixing his gaze to his left palm, he closed his fingers around the tiny wounds. The idea of another plant tunneling into his flesh frightened him. "I don't know. I'll see what I can do…" maybe there was another way. Cookies were his weakness after all. A mischievous grin pulled on his face. "It will cost you though." He motioned for her to hand over the other bag. "Ok fine here, but I hope it is worth the payment." Isaac snatched the bag and immediately plunged his hand inside for a cookie. He lifted one up to examine. Holding it to his nose he sniffed it, then licked it before biting into it. He looked at her, disgust on his face. "Hey these aren't oatmeal cookies!"

"No, they're chocolate chip. So what a cookie's a cookie."

Isaac's face fell. He placed the half eaten cookie back into the bag, rolled it shut, and handed it back to her. "Next time bring oatmeal." For a moment Sam thought he'd refuse to help her, but instead he stuffed her plant into his sweatshirt and nodded his pardon. "See ya…Come back later. Okay." He headed off into the forest without a backward glance. Sam stood holding the bag of cookies, staring after him. "Picky isn't he?" She turned her wrist over and frowned. It was almost three in the afternoon. It wouldn't be long before she had to meet up with her 'client'. This was going to be a long day.

Isaac sat in the middle of the forest staring at the sickly plant while Sedrick hopped around it on thin black legs. "Well, what do you say boy. Should I give it a try?" The little bird gave a happy chirp. "Ok, let's see what I can do." Pushing back his sleeves, he cupped his hands around the plant. Closing his eyes, he visualized the plant getting better. After a few seconds his eyes opened. "Nothing, I did it just as Wisty taught me", his light blue lip slipped out and he set the plant back on the dirt. "I don't get it." He folded his arms and stared at it, "so what do you want?" he asked the plant a little flustered. His mind drifted back to the walnut; unfolding his arms he examined the scar on his left palm. He swallowed hard. "Well if it will help you get better…" hesitantly he placed his index finger in his mouth, stopping just shy of biting down when he heard Wisteria's voice. "Porty what on earth are you doing?" Isaac looked up into Wisteria's withered face, absently leaving his finger perched between his sharp white teeth. She was glaring at him. "I fall asleep for a few minutes and you take off! I know it doesn't take that long to get wa…ter…" She stumbled over her words as she peered down at the sickly plant between the boy's feet. A distinct and over powering sweet smell hit her nose. Wisteria's breath caught in her throat, as she took a step back. Isaac looked at the terrified face of the old woman, as she backed away from him. "What's the matter?" She tore her terrified gaze from the plant to lock eyes with the boy "Where did you get that?" she stammered pointing a shaky finger at the wilting orchid. Isaac cocked his head to one side wondering what all the fuss was about. "A girl asked me to fix it, but I don't think I can. I tried doing it like you taught me, but it didn't work. Do you think you could…?" He lifted the plant up to her in hopes she'd take it. "No! Don't touch that!" She snatched the plant from him and threw it into the woods. "Wisty? What did you do that for?" Wisteria did not hear him. Her eyes were dark and wide. Her breath was short and quick. Isaac stood up and placed his hands on her shoulders. "Wisty are you ok?" She twisted out of his grip and violently slapped him on the cheek. "Why did you bring that here?!"

Isaac placed a cool hand on his stinking skin. "She asked me to help; it's important to her." He continued rubbing the burn left behind by the force of her strike. Growing impatient, Wisteria grabbed his wrist and pulled it away from his face. "So, you'll help a girl you barely know, but you won't help your own people even though that plant…" Isaac wrenched his arm free tears threatening to fall from his lashes, "you don't get it! She's real and she's important to me. Shouldn't she be important to you too? After all she is your daughter." Turning from her he ran after the plant. Wisteria stared at his back unable to order him to stop. Pressure built in her chest, constricting her throat; her body convulsed and she slumped to the ground. She held the contents of her stomach back by clamping her hand tightly over her mouth. "A girl? …. How… it's been nearly 70 years…?"

Ch. 8

"Our great protector,

will aid the faithful"

Sam knocked at the office door, waiting for permission to enter. Marco sat back comfortably in a low velvet chair while, Mr. B leaned on the desk his hands folded in front of him as of if in prayer. His bulbous eyes were locked on Marco. When the door creaked opened and Sam stepped inside,

Marco stood to greet her. "Sammie my chicka!…Would you look at that Mr. B." Marco spread his arms wide like some game show bimbo showing off a new car. Mr. B nodded his round head which looked like a bob because his fat neck didn't provide much of a fulcrum. Sam shifted nervously under Marco's penetrating gaze. He just wouldn't look away. The idea of what she was supposed to do tonight was unsettling; it felt like someone had unleashed earthworms in her stomach. The look she received from Marco sent them into a frenzy. "I'm impressed my chicka. There is hope for you yet, what do you say Mr. B? I think your client will be very pleased!" Marco stepped in leaning a little closer to Sam's ear. "If you're lucky Sammie you can be paid in full by tonight." His breath sent shivers down her spine. She didn't want to think about what this client wanted, her mind felt hazy. *I feel ill, I don't know if I can go through with this.* This thought she kept to herself, what she said conveyed none of her weakness to Marco. "Yeah, sure whatever. The sooner I get this over with the better."
Knock Knock

Mr. B's buggy eyes darted towards the dark wooden door. "Come in Mr. Philips! Your girl is all dolled up and ready to be your sweetheart for the evening." His thick black lips pulled back into a leer as his eyes roamed over Sam. She tried to ignore him. The door opened revealing a rather tiny man with hunched narrow shoulders; he was barely taller than her. His skin was dark, and rough like he had spent too much time in the sun. In this case, the dark skin was thanks to a tanning bed; the white circles around his eyes were a dead giveaway. His face webbed into a map of premature wrinkles as he smiled. Sam cringed; it was like looking at a younger and creepier version of her foster father. She clenched her eyes shut in an attempt to block the nightmare from returning. Her eyes shot open at his voice, which was high pitched and scratchy. "Well, Mr. B you never do disappoint…where did you find this one?" *At least that isn't the same,* she thought. No her foster father's voice had been low and harsh except when he whispered into her ear at night. Then it was smooth and slippery like the slug he was. Just thinking about the past made her skin crawl. The man smiled as his grey eyes hovered at her bare arms then traveled along her collar bone to rest on her bony chin. "Yes I do like this one she's a bit tall for my taste, but what a magnificent jaw line." Sam was starting to feel like a sirloin that was being tossed to a homeless man. "Well my dear shall we...." Luckily her goose bumps were misinterpreted. He thought his good looks were giving her chills and that was the only invitation he needed. Mr. Philips crossed the room in a flash and attempted to grip her by the arms. Out of reflex, Sam smacked the man's hands aside. As soon as she did, she regretted it. A sharp sting set the side of her cheek on fire. The cold metal was all too familiar. "You ungrateful bitch!" Marco withdrew his hand a second before Mr. B reprimanded him "Enough!" He looked from Sam to Marco. "Don't be damaging the merchandise before our honor client has a chance to break it him for himself." Sam wasn't too fond of being called 'it' but thought better of complaining. Mr. B turned his yellowed eyes back towards Sam. "... Girl I suggest you mind your manners." The look he gave her was enough to confirm she had made the right choice by staying quiet. This was the first time Sam really had to deal with Mr. B, but it didn't take long for her to figure out she shouldn't cross him. She nodded tentatively. "Good child, now go out and have a good time", he cued like a father sending his daughter off to prom, as if this were voluntary.

The evening air hit his lungs cool and crisp. The leaves jumped into the air as he swung his feet through the debris. It felt good to run through the woods. He remembered the days when Wisteria wouldn't even let him leave camp. She demanded that he stay and train. Her eye sight had deteriorated over the years, allowing him a chance to escape into the woods. It was never for long. She would always find him and drag him back for more cruel instructions. Then one day he discovered the city; it was a place Wisteria dared not tread. It quickly became his sanctuary. There were so many things he loved about it. There was no training, no bugs for breakfast, and no Wisteria telling him what he could and couldn't do. He continued walking; brushing fallen branches aside with his foot and tipping rocks over, for the fun of it. He had to admit being little surprised at how far into the woods he had traveled. Camp was lost from view. For such an old lady, she sure had one hell of a throwing arm. Sederick chirped in the air, circling something on the ground ahead, then landed near a plant that looked to have been up rooted. "Good job Sederick!"

The bird blinked his little eyes up at Isaac. Leaning over Isaac, gingerly picked up the plant. "Well I guess it's okay." Wiping the dirt from its leaves, he placed it back in its pot. He had found the pot a few feet from camp. "Should we head back now?" Sedrick nodded curtly and fluttered up to rest on the boy's shoulder.

"NO! Get off me!" The bird leapt up in alarm, landing on a branch overhead, it chattered profusely at the sprite prince. "That wasn't me boy", Isaac protested. Isaac's ears twitched as the scream echoed through the woods. He tucked the plant into his hoody and ran in the direction of the cry of protest. "Sedrick go ahead of me." The blue bird dove from the branch flying into the distance.

As the woods thinned in front of him, he could see a girl with long blonde hair under the halo of a lamp post. She was backing away from an undersized slender man in a business suit. The girl managed to put a few feet between herself and the man, but he quickly closed the gap grabbing her arm and pulling her into his chest. "Let me go you perv!" she screamed. "Come now. We both knew the arrangements. It wasn't like you didn't expect this." She shoved at his chest, but the man refused to let her go. "No, this was not the arrangement", she shot back. "Now, now, sweetheart Mr. B told you, that you could earn up the money in just a night or two... depending on my satisfaction of course. That isn't so bad is it?"

The girl's body relaxed slightly in the man's arms. He leaned in nibbling her chin and jaw then moved down her neck. Her body stiffened as his hands moved from around her waist to her breast. Her heart desperately tried to escape the cage of her chest. Adrenaline sent a surge of power to her legs and her knee shot up connecting hard into the man's crotch. He released her with a yelp and doubled over cupping his tender jewels. While his form was still curled over, Sam took the opportunity to run. Forcing his body up right in spite of the pain, the man reached out snatching the loose fabric of her shirt sending her to the ground. She tried to regain her balance but had managed to catch her ankle in a hole twisting it, falling face first into the dirt. The man seemed to have recovered and was now advancing on her. She had turned around facing him and began inching away.

"You little bitch. Just for that I'll have my way with you every night until I'm satisfied before I even pay a portion of your debt." A twisted grin pulled at his lips as he straddled above her. He locked her wrist in an iron grip over her head with one hand. Using his free hand, he unbuckled his belt. He stopped suddenly when he felt a light tap to the back of his head, "Hey who threw that?"

Sam stared past him. There was no one there. Mr. Philips felt another thump but this time it was much harder; a gulf-ball-sized rock rolled by his feet. "Ouch! Stop that…come out here and face me like a man you punk!" As he stood up his pants fell around his ankles. While he scanned the park for the interloper, Sam pushed herself away never taking her eyes off Mr. Philips. Something slithered from behind the man and crawled into the pool of his pants. Sam watched in amazement as it shifted around like a snake. She felt something tug at her arm pulling her attention away from the creature moving around the man's ankles. "What?" Sam looked into wide aqua colored eyes. "Shh…", Isaac pressed a slender finger to his blue lips and helped her up. He pulled her away. The man turned back to make sure his captive hadn't gotten far. He watched as a small boy drug the girl into the woods. "Hey punk what do you think…?" He reached down to pull up his pants, but they wouldn't budge. He tried to free his legs from the material but it held firm. "What the hell is going on here?" Something green slithered up his leg, "Snake!" He started beating at it with his fists and attempted to pry it off.

Isaac looked back briefly, than tugged lightly on Sam's wrist. "That won't hold him for long. Come on!" Sam allowed the boy to lead her into the woods and away from the screaming man. The forest around her disappeared as she stared at the back of the boy's spiky head, and down to the hand guiding her. He had long slender fingers that led back to a narrow wrist. Wrapped around

it was a rope like bracelet. Two tear shaped beads
dangling from it. She peeled her eyes from her
rescuer to look back over her shoulder. She could
still hear the man shouting after them…."GET
BACK HERE YOU PUNK….I PAID GOOD
MONEY FOR THAT ONE!" Flustered the man
stopped trying to wiggle free. He realized, he
wasn't being held by a snake after all and fished a
knife from his pants pocket in order to cut away
the vines. "I wouldn't bother." His irritated eyes
peered over his shoulder to see an old withered
woman standing only a few feet away. She was
smoking a long pipe with weird greenish smoke
whisping from the end. Stepping in closer, she
blew a cloud of the thick sweet smoke into his
face. "Sorry…but, old hags are just not my thi…",
before he could finish his sarcastic remark, he
collapsed convulsing on the ground. "Rotten
smelling humans aren't my thing either." She
tipped the remaining powder from the end of her
pipe over the man's face and turned to leave.
Stopping briefly, she looked up into the lamp
light; a small blue bird was perched at the top.
"Come on you annoying water imp. I have a little
twerp to scold." Sedrick flew down from the lamp

post after Wisty, leaving the man sprawled on the ground in a pool of his own vomit and drool.

"Hey, let me go already!" Isaac looked back along his arm to the girl, he had drug half way through the forest as if he just remembered she was there. He blinked past silver lashes, "you look different." Sam felt the heat rise in her checks and quickly pulled her wrist free from the boy's grip. Once free, she immediately regretted it; pain shot up her leg and she crumbled to the ground holding her sore ankle. "Damn it!" Isaac cocked his head, watching her rock back and forth as she held her ankle. "Are you ok?" Sam shot him a look "No stupid, I'm not. You just dragged me half way through the forest on a sprained ankle!" She leaned back taking the pressure off her right foot. Making the mistake of looking down at her clothing, she grew even more annoyed. She pinched her silk shirt between her forefinger and thumb grumbling, "Great my outfit is ruined too…how am I supposed to pay for this? Ugh, you should have just left me there. Now I owe Mr. B even more money!" Without a word Isaac dropped to his knees in front of her, and roughly pulled her leg out of her hands to examine it. Sam looked at him in surprise. "What are you…?" Slowly his fingers moved down her calf and cupped the heel of her sandal. He peeled it off and tossed it aside. "Hey!…" Her anger quelled as he wrapped his cool fingers around her ankle. She felt the heat rise in her face at the sudden intimacy. This was the closest she'd ever been to the boy. It was also the first time she saw him without his hood pulled up around his face. Even though it was dark, she could see that his features were somewhat ethereal. His nose was sharp yet delicate; his lashes were long and thick they looked silver in the moonlight; his lips were thin and pale blue; and his skin was a smooth shadowed tan. Isaac felt her eyes searching his face; blood warm and tingly *whished* through his ears. He lifted his gaze up into her curious caramel pools, than quickly looked away. Lowering her foot gently, he stood up. He tossed his hood back up over his head and glanced down at her briefly. She felt so awkward; had she offended him? "Um…Sorry I just…"He stumbled over his words making only brief eye contact before heading out of the clearing. "Hey, wait!…", she called after

116

him."…I guess he doesn't like people looking at him," she mumbled to herself.

Looking around, she realized for the first time since her rescue that she had no idea where she was, or how to get back. "Isaac get back here you jerk! How am I supposed to get home?!" Hearing a rustle from the trees, she immediately turned assuming the boy had returned. The moment of hope was fleeting as it turned to disappointment the second she saw the small blue bird enter the clearing. It landed near her carrying a tiny pouch. "For me?" The bird hopped over dropping it into her awaiting palm. "Um thank you…I think…but, uh what's it for?"…."Your ankle." She turned toward the voice. It was dry and cracked. "If you wrap that around your ankle you should be able to walk home…the pigeon will show you the way out." Sam looked up into an ancient face frozen in a scowl. Hiding behind it was Isaac, his hood casting his face in shadows. He lowered his head, and turned away. He stopped briefly to apologize to Sam before he was ordered to go back to camp. "I'm sorry Sam I have to go now." Sam tried to stop him. "Isaac, wait…" Wisteria stepped forward blocking him from view. "He is none of

117

your concern girlie. Now go home". Sam watched his head fall in resignation before he ran into the darkness. "Isaac!" she called after him. Attempting to stand and challenge the old hag, Sam's ankle gave out the instant she put weight on it. "Want to try that again girl?...I suggest you wrap up that ankle and leave." Wisteria stood firm like a bouncer between a crazed fan and the rock star. "You best forget that boy and go back to your own life." Wisteria didn't budge from her sentry until Sam wrapped her ankle and hobbled out of the forest following her feathered guide.

Ch. 9

"A woman of stranger's blood

will bare our savior"

   *knock knock *
"Un what…who is it?" Sam rolled over, tugging
her night shirt down over her underwear and
slipping her feet into a pair of old slippers before
shuffling over to the door.
knock knock

"Who the hell would knock on my door this early in the morning?" She pushed a lever opening a vent in the door to peer out. "Whoever it is certainly is short", she grumbled. Unable to see who it was she yelled, "Go away!"

"Sam...Sam may I come in?" "Isaac?" Sam peeked through the door to find Isaac bundled in several blankets shivering at her door step. "What are you doing here and how do you know where I live?" Isaac just pointed up to a blue bird sitting on the railing. "Ah, my little escort and how are you this morning?" Sam asked a little sarcastically. The bird didn't respond. "Fine don't tell me." Isaac sneezed and Sam ushered him inside. "Would you two get in already before you freeze on my steps and someone sees you." Once inside Isaac dropped his warm covers. His eyes scanned the room and immediately fell on the line of plastic trays at the back. Stepping over to the seedlings, he peered down into the dirt. "So you grow your own vegetables or something?" Sam flushed, "no..um I mean they're sort of for work." He turned back blinking at her. "Work?" Sam looked away rubbing the back of her arm. Feeling a little exposed she spied Lewie's dress shirt laying on the bed and dove for it. It'd at least give her a bit more cover then her oversized t-shirt. Once wrapped in it she sat at the end of her cot avoiding eye contact and mumbled, "Yeah, um remember when I told you I lost my stash, and I got beat up for it. Well that is its replacement. If I don't get them to grow into full sized plants by next week…" She lifted her head and forced a smile "…well I guess I'll be having a lot more nights like last night." Isaac's brow dropped into a scowl. "I don't think you should see people like that anymore." Sam looked away, staring down at the light blue sleeve of Lewie's dress shirt. "Well it isn't like I want to", she protested "I just don't have a choice right now." Isaac turned from Sam and looked down at the plants. "So if these plants are full grown you won't have to see people like that man anymore?" Sam avoided his awaiting gaze and said sheepishly, "Something like that.".… Isaac rolled up his sleeves and placed each finger into his mouth. "Ok then." Sam stared at him in shock. "Wait, what are you do…ing?" She watched as he bit down on each finger until a small bead of blood rested on the tips; then he buried his hands into the dirt. "Grow", he commanded. Within seconds the seedlings began to grow. Sam watched in amazement as they grew taller and fuller.

Something moved outside causing a shadow to fall over Isaac's back. Sam shot up from her cot and quickly stepped between the shadow and Isaac. Isaac didn't seem to notice. She leaned in close as the seedlings pushed their way up, expanding from the dirt like sponges, as they soaked up Isaac's blood. "Wow... how did you do that?" Isaac pulled his hands from the dirt, brushing the remaining bits back into the pots. "I'm not really allowed to say ahem.." He felt the heat rise in his entire body as he felt her soft chest push against his back... "Um... Wisteria gets angry with me enough already" he pulled his sleeves back down and slipped from under her intimate contact. Sam blinked at his sudden discomfort, then shrugged. "Oh! You mean that old woman?" Placing some distance between himself and Sam he nodded. "Yeah, she's kinda like my aunt."..."Doesn't your mom or dad have a say in what you do and who you speak to? Why do you have to listen to her?" Isaac's face turned sad and he looked away. "My mother is dead and

I've never met my father." Sam blushed and turned her attention back to the plants. "Oh well… I'm sorry I brought it up." Isaac held up his hand and shook his head, "No its ok. I don't remember her anyway. She died when I was just a baby. Besides I came to tell you I can't fix your plant so I wanted to give it back to you." He pulled the blue sickly flower from his jacket and handed it to Sam. "Here" Sam looked down at it in dismay. "I guess you can only do what you can." Isaac watched as the disappointment pulled at her features. She looked as if someone had just told her best friend died. Shoving his hands in his pocket he looked about the stone walls, "Anyway, I'd better go now. She'll be looking for me", he turned to leave trying to avoid the sad puppy face Sam was giving him over the plant. "Wait a second Isaac I… never mind…" Isaac shrugged and reached for the door…."No wait!" He turned around a little irritated but listened. Sam looked anxious. "Don't go out the front. Maybe you should slip out the back door so no one sees." He raised a brow at this, but did as she suggested. Once he was safely out the back Sam ran to the front and checked down the street. "Good, I swear I saw someone standing there."

The steel door gave with a slight shove and he covered his eyes as the light spilled across the room to greet him. He crossed the room to a small nightstand; a vase full of pink and white flowers sat on top. He picked the lilies up and took them into the bathroom for some water. *These are beautiful I thought it was too late in the year for Lilies.* A frail voice followed him into the bathroom. "They're lovely aren't they… he came by to see me again… I must have frightened him so…I was hoping I could tell him I was okay." When Lewie returned, the woman was sitting up staring out the window. "Who mother?" Cary just smiled. "You know, the boy I spoke of so frequently. He's such a tender hearted thing. I must have made him worry so." Lewie set the flowers on the table then reached out to pat his mother's hand. "Yes you gave us all quite a scare; how are you feeling today?" Cary turned her wary eyes up into her son's. "Just fine. Nothing to worry about" Lewie smiled and pulled the chair up beside the bed than reached out taking her hand. "That's wonderful…what have the doctors said about your progress?" Cary shifted her weight and turned back towards the window. "Nothing new really…they say the same thing to me every day… 'we can't find anything that is causing your heart failure, but we will continue to run test'" she stated in a matter-of-fact way. Sighing she looked at her son, and took his hand in both of hers. "Louis honey I am glad that you have found Sam, but finding her is not enough. I owe that poor girl for the life she had to live for so many years…after your father died I truly wanted to make amends and adopt her, but she had already been picked up by a farmer's family. I thought everything was working out for her…but" her voice dropped. "I wish I had looked into the kind of environment she grew up in." Lewie patted her hand and smiled. "Don't worry mother. I'll take care of everything." Her face twisted as if she suddenly remembered something, than it fell as the thought floated away again. "What is it mother?" She looked a little lost for a moment then shook her head, "It's nothing, don't worry about it...Sweetheart I'm getting a little tired could you come visit later? I'd appreciate it." Cary leaned back and closed her eyes. A weak smile tugged at the corner of his lips and he reached down to pull the covers up over the elder woman. "Take care mother." He squeezed her hand gently then left the hospital. *I'm sorry mother. I know that boy means something to you, but I don't see any other way. I have to do this for Sam.*

Isaac strolled back into camp just after dawn. Wisteria was curled up under her wool shawl snoring peacefully. Creeping up, he knelt down in front of her. "Wisty... psst Wisty... are you awake?"...."Ggggrrrr" Isaac looked over at

Sedrick then back to Wisteria, "Jeez, she's even grumpy in her sleep."…"Wisteria, wake up its morning. I'm ready to train now." One wrinkled lid crept opened to peer cynically at the boy. "What's the joke about boy? You trying to pull something? Want to negotiate do you?" Isaac stepped away from her accusing eyes. "No I just want to learn." He objected. "Sure you do…and what do you want to learn?" Isaac looked about nervously. Had she figured him out, could she tell he had ulterior motives? His eyes focused on the crisp ends of a burnt leaf, swaying at the end of a branch, sticking out of the fire. "Lots of things like, how to heal burnt leaves, and treat fungus and… how to save a dying plant" his voice lowered at the last bit. Both the old woman's eyes shot open. "Ah ha, so that's what this is all about. You want to save that girl's plant don't you?" Isaac did his best to look hurt, "No, of course not but you said it yourself, I'm the only one who can fix them so…" Wisteria scrutinized his resolve then reluctantly agreed. "Fine, we'll start with fungus." Not one of Isaac's favorites but it least he was getting somewhere.

127

"No, no not like that, if you keep going about it like that you're bound to end up with athlete's foot or something." Isaac was kneeling barefoot in the dirt holding a moldy looking plant by the tips of its leaves. Its fuzzy roots extended down desperately groping for the purple liquid pooling under Isaac's foot. His head was cocked to one side as he attempted to bite into the plants stem. Wisteria held back a snort of laughter; he looked ridiculous. The face he was making wasn't helping the matter. His features were scrunched up into a pucker and drool poured from his lower lip, as the plant's bitter liquid squished between his teeth. "Yuck!" Wisteria couldn't contain the laughter. "Ka ka ha ha… how is what you're doing anything like I said boy?" Isaac dropped the plant and stood up, crest fallen. Once again he had gotten it all wrong. He was only supposed to give it a tiny bit of his own blood to bolster the plants immunity then suck and spit the 'poison' out. Instead he was chewing on the stem making faces with each bite. He was also sporting an opened wound at the top of his foot that only served to feed the plants already growing in the ground. "But you said feed with your feet and eat its poison." "That's not what I said boy...you weren't paying attention" She snatched the plant off the ground and pointed toward the stream. "Go take care of your foot already. You seem to be better with that sort of thing anyway". Isaac looked down at his foot, then back up to the disappointed amber orbs. *I really am no good at this.*

By the time Isaac returned, Wisteria had already set up another challenge for him. "Here, this one is just sickly. It has had poor soil and not enough water. It shouldn't take much for you to fix it. Now just give it a little blood and command that blood where it needs to go inside the plant." Isaac nodded, "So just like helping a plant grow then?" Wisteria nodded. "Precisely..." Isaac took the plant gingerly in his hands and allowed it to have access to his veins. "Now remember feel it's pulse, and match yours to it" she instructed. The tentacles moved through him. He could feel its rhythm align with his own. The deeper the plant dove the more nervous he became. His heart rate jumped and the plant fed with fervor on his blood. Its yellow leaves darkened into a rich green, its stem shot up, and the plant began to overflow from his hands. "Stop, you are too nervous you're giving it too much…do you want it to drain you dry?" Wisteria ripped the plant from his hands. "Maybe we should start with bonding before you go out handing over your blood like candy on Halloween." Isaac looked confused. "Bonding?" The old woman lowered her head shaking it slowly from side to side, a deep sigh escaped her lips. "You have to learn to bond with a plant so that there is a mutual respect. If you're not careful it will take advantage of you." Isaac swallowed hard and nodded, "I can do this. Just give me another chance." Wisteria eyed him incredulously, "You've done enough today, why don't you go visit that woman in the hospital or something? I'm sure she would like to see you." Wisteria watched as the boy's face lit up and wondered if giving him permission was a mistake. "Be back here before night fall Porty, or I will make it impossible for you to go out ever again." He nodded his understanding, than motioned for Sedrick to follow him. "Wait I need you to leave that bird here. I could use him today." The two exchanged glances. The old sprite had never desired the bird's company for anything before. Isaac shrugged and waved goodbye to his friend. "Um ok, I'll see you later then"

Sedrick watched as the boy left, then with a bit of hesitation flew over to Wisteria. He landed on a branch eye level to the old woman. Two sets of eyes waited for the boy to vanish completely. The bird turned back to Wisteria…*What could you possibly want with me Wisteria?* "It's just a hunch. I need you to go check on that girl he's been hanging around." *I hardly owe you any favors Wisty,* the bird snapped back. "Oh you don't do you… how do you suppose you escaped that mansion sixty years ago?" Wisteria retorted. Sedrick looked flustered and fluffed his feathers. *Fine but you should learn to trust that boy more often…he has a good heart. He just doesn't understand his destiny. Personally if I could prevent his fate I would.* Wisteria looked insulted…"Do you honestly believe I want that boy to die… he is like a son to me. I wish I could think of a way to help our brethren without having to sacrifice him." The blue bird shook its tiny head. *I honestly don't think you try hard enough. For saplings sake can't a water sprite and a wood sprite together do the same job as the prince?* Wisteria looked thoughtful. "You have a point; however, do you know of any wood sprites around here that have not been cursed?" She said the last bit jamming a thumb into her chest, indicating herself. Sedrick lowered his head and shook it lightly. *I suppose not.* "Right now go look in on that girl already. No sense standing around here…. Off with ya."

In the basement of the club Sam was being given the royal treatment. That is of course, if she was part of an enemy country. Marco paced the floor downing one bottle of water after another. "So you have been hiding this little golden goose from me eh … chicka?" Sam twisted around in her chair unable to move freely due to the binding. "No, I'm telling you I just met him!" Marco tapped his fingers against his chin then pointed with the now empty water bottle to the row of plants along the wall. "So are you telling me Lewie is lying and he did not see this golden goose of yours, make these things grow?" Sam shot Lewie a reproachful look. "I don't know what you're talking about. It must be the new fertilizer." Marco wasn't convinced, "I see, and did you not tell me just the other day you were out of supplies?" Sam looked lost. She wasn't sure how to cover for Isaac now. "Sammie, Sammie, Sammie don't lie to me... you know I hate liars." Marco's hand swung back and Sam squeezed her eyes shut and steadied herself for the blow. After a second when it hadn't come, she pried her lids open to find Lewie's arm pressed against Marco's. "Marco instead of beating Sam up for this, why don't we just use her to get the kid; he's obviously more useful than her." It was as if Lewie himself had struck her instead of Marco. How could he? She had trusted him. "Cat you jerk! I can't believe..." Lewie quickly threw his other hand over her mouth, glancing at her briefly, before turning back to Marco. Lewie then led Marco out of earshot of the girl. Their bodies so close together Sam could only see a few glances in her direction. The men finally parted with Marco jabbing a finger at Lewie's chest. "Fine, but you have two days Lewie. That is all this stash will last us...you got that? Two days!" A nervous grin twitched into place. "Not a problem Marco." Sam was so angry she couldn't look at the man she had trusted for so long. "Take care of her", was Marco's last order before slamming the door on Lewie and Sam. They were finally alone. "What the hell were you thinking...I can't believe you told Marco about Isaac! I swear, if anything happens to him I'll never forgive you Lewie. Never!" Louis Valentino bent down level with the girl and loosened her binding. "Listen to me Sam, I have thought of every possible way to get you out of this situation and I couldn't find an answer. Marco would chase you to the ends of the earth, you know that. He won't let his little money maker just up and leave. Then I saw the boy. You could be free. You wouldn't have to work for Marco ever again." Iridescent tears streamed down her face. Once her hands were free she slapped him. "Cat how could you...I know you are just trying to protect me, but how could you just sacrifice him like that. Don't you feel any remorse at all?" Lewie stood up and turned his back on her. "I'm sorry Sam, but blood is thicker than water." Sam stopped wiping her tears to give Lewie a bewildered look. "What are you talking

134

about?" He spun around taking her hand, "I think there is someone you should meet."

Isaac was practically skipping. He had been given permission to go into the city; no worries over getting an earful when he came back. It felt wonderful. He knew he was supposed to go visit Cary in the hospital, but he had to make a quick stop first. After all she hadn't told him not to visit Sam. Turning the corner of Maple then up 13th Street he stopped in front of a flight of concrete steps. Hopping down them he freed his hand from his front pocket then tapped lightly on the peeling wooden door. "Sam…Sam are you home?" …He couldn't wait to tell her. He knew how to fix her plant now, or at least he thought he did. "Sam?" He knocked a little harder this time and the door creaked open. "Oh good Sam I'm…" There was no one. The door had merely swung open under inertia. It was dark inside except for the small amount of light coming through the narrow back windows. "I wonder where?..." He looked about until his eyes settled on the sickly blue flower. "Ah well at least I found you, come on I think I can fix you now." He gently tucked the plant into his sweatshirt, closed the door securely behind him and then made his way toward the hospital.

Ch. 10

Sam stared down several stories to the concrete walk below; her smooth forehead pressed against the cold glass. "So basically you're trying to tell me I am… not human…or something right?" Cary pushed herself up in bed with a little assistance from her son. She rested a weary hand on his. "Please, Louis I'm all right." She swung her legs around and tossed the blanket aside setting her bare feet down onto the cold tile. "Samantha...I was asked not to say anything to you...your mother didn't want you to know...she wanted you to grow up as a normal human girl. Nothing more, she just did what she thought was best for you." Sam spun around to face the woman's frail eyes, "Normal girl...you mean to tell me bouncing from one home to another, than back to the orphanage, then finally ending up at some sick-o's farm was the life of a normal girl...?! Why didn't she just keep me?" Choking on sobs, she turned her back on the woman, desperate to keep the tears from falling. Sam lost the battle; an iridescent tear broke free and slid down her cheek. "Samantha?... do you still have that plant you got from the orphanage?" Sam quickly wiped the warm liquid from her cheek. "No it was injured and I gave it to Isaac to fix." Cary's hand flew up to her chest. "Isaac!" Cary spun around to her son as a look of complete panic spread across her features; her breath came in short gasps. Lewie was instantly by her side.

"Mom are you all right?"

Sam jumped in interrupting Lewie's concern, "Wait so you know Isaac?" Cary turned dull brown eyes towards Sam. A withered smile clung to her face, "I met him many years ago I was only twenty Louis had not even been conceived yet." She turned from Sam and reached a knobby hand up to clutch at her son's sleeve. "Louis you have to get that plant away from him. It was never meant for him." Lewie looked a little confused, "Mom please, calm down. You don't want to have another attack. I'm sure it's fine. It's just a plant after all", he said as he tried to get her to lay back down. Sam's voice came softly from the other side of the bed, her head down. "It doesn't matter. He couldn't fix it he brought it back to me the other day." The old woman's eyes scanned the girl for candor, when she was satisfied the girl spoke the truth her breath returned to normal and she felt the tightness in her chest subside. "I'm all right Louis" she waved Lewie's supportive arms away, and motioned for Sam to sit beside her. She took a deep breath before speaking again, as if to prepare herself for the girl's reaction. "Samantha your mother gave me that plant to pass on to you as a means of keeping your mixed blood a secret." Sam tossed a hand up, effectively stopping the old woman's story.

"Wait…you said something about that earlier. So you knew my mother, but why…and what did you mean by a mix of blood? First you tell me I may not be human, now you tell me I'm a mix…a mix of what?" Cary took another deep breath and looked the girl directly in the eyes. "Your father was human…your father was…my husband and Louis's father." Sam felt the room spin and her knees gave in. All this time she had a brother right beside her. "You mean…Lewie and I are…but….how…I thought…" Cary looked away a little ashamed for tricking the girl. "I'm sorry Samantha… your mother was involved with my husband long before I met him. I was very young when I met your father; he was already grey by the time we married. I knew he had a child by another woman, but complications kept them from being together. …You were born without him knowing where you and your mother had gone…I searched after his death despite his request to leave it be; however, I blamed myself for your fate. If my family had not arranged the marriage between Fredrick and me you could have grown up in a home with your mother and father. It took years to find you and when I had; it turned out you had been placed in an orphanage. I came back to this area once I discovered which orphanage was caring for you, but as I stood outside the doors of the cathedral a woman approached me and asked that we speak. That is when she gave me that plant and told me everything about you and the wood sprites. She told me to make sure the orphanage gave you the plant and that I should let you be adopted by a family that did not know of your secret so you could grow up normal from then on."

Sam still looked confused, "So what's the deal with the plant…how did that help me…why did she want me to grow up as a human anyway?" Cary hesitantly took the girl's hand, and was relieved when she did not pull away. "Samantha that plant fed off your sprite blood every night as you slept so that you would grow up like a normal girl. You went through three families as an infant before I gave that plant to the orphanage. Each family that adopted you, returned you to the orphanage after three years saying that you were bewitched because you never aged." Sam found herself staring at the palm of her hand and wondering, just how old she really was? Her light caramel eyes lifted up from her palm and into Lewie's warm brown eyes. "How long have you known?" Avoiding her gaze Lewie walked over to the window. Sam stared at his back as he crossed the room, wishing her will alone would get him to look at her. "Answer me damn it! ...Is that why you have always been there? Was I just some pet you were supposed to take care of?!...Cat, answer me!" Lewie pressed his forehead to the cool glass and sighed watching the warmth of his breath fog the window. "I didn't know until a few weeks ago, honest. ...Mother told me to watch over you, but she didn't tell me why. ...I never thought of you as some pet...I care about you that's why I watched over you as much as I could." He took another deep breath, "You don't have to believe me...but now you should consider what I told you before; get out of town while you can. Think about it, if your blood returns to full strength there is no way Marco would let you go." Sam moved her gaze from Lewie to Cary; she wondered if the old woman knew what Lewie's plans were. After all, she seemed to care for Isaac as well, but she just couldn't bring herself to disappoint the old woman, who was so full of pride for her son. "Thank you for your time ma'am. I will look after Isaac…he's special to me too." Sam squeezed Cary's hand lightly. She shot a look towards Lewie before excusing herself from the room. Lewie looked at Sam, then his mother. "I'll be back later mother. Try to get some rest ok?" Cary nodded but reached out to stop him before he left, "Louis I know you need to protect Sam, but Isaac is very important to all of us. Please, look out for the two of them." He swallowed hard and did his best to smile, "Of course mother, take care."

The glass doors slid open and Sam stormed out of the hospital onto the sidewalk Lewie stopped her by grabbing her wrist. "Sam wait please I didn't know." Sam turned to face him, hurt and anger in her eyes. "What difference does it make if he is someone your mother cares for or not; Cat you were willing to toss him in a pit of alligators, don't you feel anything?" Lewie dropped her hand, "I'm sorry Samantha."…"You are sorry, but how does that fix this? Isaac is in trouble. Marco will search for him relentlessly now he…." Something moved catching Sam's attention. She turned her head to find a boy in an oversized green hoody and worn jeans staring at the couple from beside the partition. "Isaac?" Her voice broke his trance and he turned running away from the two. "Isaac Wait!" Lewie held her firm, "let him go, talking to him now isn't going to get you anywhere. Let him calm down. I'm sure he got the wrong idea."

Sam brushed Lewie's hand away and turned to face him. "Cat you have to fix this. Marco knows about Isaac now, you heard your mother she cares for Isaac too; you can't just hand him over to Marco." Lewie's head fell in shame then he rested his large hands atop Sam's bony shoulders, looking her dead in the eye he said, "I'll fix this I promise, for now just go home ok." Sam pulled away and her eyes followed the path Isaac took. Her heart sank. She wanted to run after him, but Cat was probably right, going after him would only push him away more. "Ok fine, but be careful. I doubt Marco will give up on this without a fight." He nodded as he waved her off and they split company.

The fire light was nothing more than dim ambers as Isaac made his way back to camp. Wisteria was nowhere in sight. He released a shaky breath and plopped down in front of the old oak tree; then pulled the small blue flower from his front pocket. "I shouldn't even bother with you. It didn't look to me like she cares if you live or die" for a moment he pondered throwing it into the fire, tears weld in his eyes…. "Well are you satisfied?" a raspy voice startled him. He quickly shoved the plant back inside his hoody, and then zipped it to his neck before spinning around to come face to face with the old sprite. He leaned back from the stern dull ambers that were as cold as a dead fish boring into his skull. "Humph, what did I tell you about humans Porty?" Isaac made to inch away along the trunk but was curtly stopped by the long knobby fingers of the old woman.

"Stay away from them Porty they will only cause you pain." His sea green eyes shifted away and he mumble softly, "but she…".Wisteria pulled at his arm forcing him to look back up at her, "But she what…she's nice to you she's different…which is it… you think she actually likes you…don't make me laugh you already saw she just wants to use you that's all humans ever want of us." Fighting back the tears Isaac jumped to the girl's defense. "No! She just needed my help. I just wanted to help her." Wisteria made a face in a mock pout, "Ah whatever for? Do you like her, maybe love her well I got news for you short stuff she already has a man in her life so let it go" Isaac looked at her is shock "How do you know?" Wisteria tossed a thumb in the bird's direction. "What do you think I had your little pigeon doing while you were gone?" Isaac shot an accusing look toward Sedrick. The bird turned its head in shame. Grasping for anything to make him feel better he protested "Maybe it isn't like that?" He tried to free his arm from her grasp, but she held firm. "You don't believe me do you…well maybe I should just show you how wonderful your humans are…come with me!"

Wisteria drug Isaac through the woods her grip burning his wrist. If she had any sense of compassion she didn't show it. When Isaac slipped down a steep slope of leaves she did not wait for him to stand; she just pulled harder dragging him along until he managed to get back to his feet. They walked for what felt like eternity and when she finally stopped they were standing in front of a large tree black and hollow a mere fossil protruding from the ground. "This…" she said motioning toward the charred remains, "…is Gurrell… our protector" she said snidely "…and your prison for over two hundred years" She tossed him in the direction of the tree, "Go on say Hi!" Isaac stumbled over catching himself on the powdered black bark of a large Sycamore. It was clear to most that this tree was dead, but he could feel a pulse beneath the blackened surface. His arms started to burn but he could not pull away. Images much like his dreams flooded into his mind.

The earth crumbled beneath her feet the wind tossed her long chestnut locks into her face. She could feel her body wavering then the final push as the arrow buried itself into her shoulder. Flying from the cliff, her body twisted in midair to shelter the small bundle cradled protectively in her arms. In a language long forgotten and only understood by the trees themselves she pleaded, "Please catch us." Her fall came to an abrupt and painful halt as her back smacked into a mass of thick roots that had shot out from the cliff side. She could still hear the girl screaming from the ledge. "Rowan!" - I'm sorry Wisteria your life will be hard, but you will endure- The girl's screams were followed by the malicious remarks of the two human men that echoed down the valley. "Where did the bitch go?"... "It's too far to see, I'm sure she's smashed against a rock somewhere down there, besides even if she managed to survive that the arrow I hit her with will finish her off" The men turned around to their colleague who was holding a small girl. "At least we got one prize she'll make some rich old dame a good maid" The girl struggled desperately to free her knots of pink and violet curls from the man's hairy fist. "Let go of me! Rowan!" the girl pleaded to air around her. "Please don't leave me!" The man pulled her closer. "Yell all you want girlie she can't hear you from where she's going" -How could you leave me Rowan-

The Priestess ripped her long hair free from the twisted knobby roots and pushed herself up to check on the baby still sleeping against her chest.-You could sleep through anything couldn't you-? She turned to face the massive tree, its roots stretched deep into the valley. "Thank you Gurrell." She laid back and pulled the arrow from her shoulder she already knew it was too late. The poison was already taking affect. –I'll have to hurry- She finished weaving the strands of her hair into a thin braided rope then pulled a small satchel from her side; in it were three tear shaped black beads. She had to chance going back into the village for them, but it was worth it. They were a gift from her grandfather. He had won the favor of the mighty bird of rebirth and these small yet miraculous claws could render one impervious to the flame. Her fingers became stiff as if frozen and her eye lids would not obey her; they kept slipping closed and obstructing her vision. She held the tiny bracelet up after fixing each claw to the thin braid. "That should do it. I wish you the best my son, remember you are the blood and life of this forest…never forget your duty." She then slipped the bracelet around the boy's soft plump wrist. "That's all I can do for you now my son grow up to be strong of heart so you can return these woods to their magnificent form…I believe in you." She brushed his tuffs of soft brown hair aside and pressed her quivering lips to his smooth forehead. "I love you Isaac; be a good boy" then she leaned her head back letting the poison

consume the rest of her strength. "Please Gurrell take
good care of him and make sure he fulfills his destiny."
Her hold on the infant slacked as hairy gray tentacles
gently wrapped around the baby taking him
protectively inside the heart wood of the massive tree.
Rowan watched with hazy eyes as her son was slowly
consumed by the soft sapwood then disappeared below
the surface. "Goodbye my son"

Isaac could feel his knees give and his body
sunk to the ground, iridescent tears flowed past
his lashes and down his cheeks. "I saw her" Wisty
snorted. "Well good for you, but what good does
that do you now? She would still be around if it
wasn't for those precious humans of yours. She
can't come back you know. Only a few of us lucky
ones managed to escape her fate that night. Most
of us were enslaved including me. I spent fifty
years under one cruel master after another...." She
paused taking a deep breathe, "The others..."
spreading her arms wide she announced, "...are
here."... "This is what is left of our family. What a
wonderful way to protect us, leave us stranded in
the open unable to escape...sitting ducks" She
dropped her arms and walked over to where Isaac
was kneeling deep in the earth. Her jagged nails

dug into his scalp as she grabbed a fistful of his hair twisting it around her gnarled fingers and yanking his face up to look at her. She spit through her teeth as she spoke. "We've all been waiting for you Princy…You are the only one who can fix them; Gurrell is just a fossil now he can no longer help any of us. This…" She said glancing over to the tree in disgust "…cannot release my sister nor fix any of the others who were forced into hiding only to be tortured for centuries" She forced his vision in the direction of camp, "My sister is out there and she is dying she cannot get up and find food or clean water she suffers from a disease; she has to stay there night after night day after day feeding only on what the humans have left behind"

"Release us", *"Free us"*, *"Please set us free"*, the voices reverberated from the bark of the trees and pounded at this skull. "Stop it!" He pressed his palms into his ears, but their voices penetrated his entire body as if entering though the pores of his skin. Their voices were like poison to his blood. He could feel their despair; it was a pain like no other. It was the full sorrow of the woods. "They are dying Porty… this world the humans have

created are killing them… you can heal them"
Tears flowed down his cheeks. "No I can't…you
saw for yourself….I'm scared" Roughly she let go
of his scalp, tossing it to the side. "Sniveling punk
don't you get it, that is why you were spared that
is why your mother betrayed us all protecting
only you, which is why Gurrell gave his entire
body to protect you" She sneered down at him in
disgust then tossed a glance over to the
Sycamore's remains. "Some savior you have been
guarding all these years; I bet now you wish I
hadn't set you on fire to release that boy" She
jabbed a crocked finger in Isaac's direction. "Fifty
years for nothing" she snorted then left the
Sycamore and the boy behind. *What?* For a
moment Isaac dropped his hands he could barely
make out what the old woman had said to Gurrell
"She released me?" The voices started in again
cries of pain and sorrow penetrated his skull like
arrows. Isaac clutched his ears trying to block
their pleas. "I… can't I'm sorry…" He pushed
himself from the earth and ran as far as he could
from the painful pleas, but no matter how far he
ran only more cries of pain crashed down upon

him. The forest was filled with the crystallized forms of his ancestors. "STOP IT!"

A.J. Zanders

Ch. 11

"The child of mix blood will be imprisoned."

Isaac's breath fogged in front of him as he stood in total darkness. He scanned his surroundings, but all that he found was blackness. A light flickered in the distance and he stepped toward it. With each step the light grew brighter until it burst into a scorching blue flame. He jump back in surprise only to hit his back into something hard. "What…sorry" just as he tried to step away something wrapped around his arms holding him firm. "What? Why can't I…" The flames rolled closer he could feel its heat he wanted desperately to run, but the dark coarse fingers only tightened against him. "Let go of me!" The tentacles inched slowly down his hoody and beneath his t-shirt "No stop it!" He felt its fuzzy fingers brush along his chest sending goose bumps up his neck. Its tiny hairs started to burrow under his skin. The deeper they buried themselves the stiffer his limbs began to feel. "Stop it! I can't move…why won't they listen to me?" He tried to reach up to free himself but his fingers had become rigid and his skin jagged. Flakes of bark broke free from his knuckles as the flames licked at his hands. His mouth opened into a silent scream, "NO!"

His sea green eyes snapped opened to a bright milky haze. The moon was a brilliant white globe in the backdrop of the night sky. Sweat slid down his temples until the freezing night air crystallized it to his jaw. *How did I get here?* He wanted to reach up and rub his arms, but he couldn't move. His entire body felt like lead. *Why can't I move?* His eyes traveled over a large grey stone behind him then down to his arm; small green sprigs curled around his sleeve. *I see I'm still dreaming.* His head rolled back to rest on the hard surface and his lids slipped closed.

Sam rolled over on her side to look out the narrow windows of her apartment. The sky was still a pale purple. She sighed and rolled back over. *What am I supposed to do?* Her mind kept drifting to Isaac; how could she keep him out of Marco's clutches. Even the incident at the park was forgotten and the need to pay back Mr. B, all she could think of was a way to save Isaac. She rolled back over facing the empty milk crate by the door.

Her eyes widened. "Wait! Where did it go?" She swung her feet around and walked over to the empty crate. Picking it up, she looked around it, and then tossed it aside. "Don't tell me…"

Remembering what Cary had told her; she crossed the room pulling the covers from her bed and tossed them to the floor; nothing. "Where is it?" She stormed over to the metal watering can picked it up and dumped its contents; water trickled from the end, but no plant. Dropping the can, it fell with a plunk.

"Where the hell?" *tap…tap…tap..* The soft sound brought her attention up to the long narrow windows; a small blue bird was sitting on the ledge. "You?" Sam walked over opening the door; the bird flew in circling around her head and began picking at her hair then swooped back out again. "Crazy bird what was that about?" She placed a hand on the door to push it closed; the bird dove through the crack and circled her room before pecking at her again. "Jeez what is it with you?" Sedrick flew from the girl to the door and began fluttering anxiously around the frame. "Stupid bird you are the one who wanted in, in the first place" she reached out opening the door to let the frantic bird back outside, but the bird did not leave. It stood at the top of the door staring down at the top of Sam's spiky green hair. "Do you want me to follow you?" Sedrick hopped up fluttering around her then back to the top of the door. "Ok ok I get it…I'll go with you." Grabbing her coat, she followed the bird out the back, down the alley and around to the courthouse. In front of the building was a large concrete memorial surrounded by flowers. The front was well groomed and manicured, but the other side seemed to have been left to over grow. "If you brought me out here to see this…it really isn't my problem why don't you crap on the guys at the courthouse." She turned to head back to her apartment when she heard a faint whimper. She stopped, taking in a deep breath of the crisp air feeling it stab at her lungs, she let her shoulders fall then turned back toward the stone. "So you had me come out her to rescue a dog huh…?"

  Sedrick hopped along the arc of the stone peering down behind it then back to the girl. Stepping over to the stone, Sam took care not to startle the animal. "You are one crazy bird what am I supposed to do with a…", "…dog?" Huddled on the other side of the stone was a boy wearing a green hooded sweat-shirt. The hood was pulled up around his ears his arms wrapped tightly around his stomach. "Isaac what are you doing

159

here?" She pulled off her coat throwing it over his frame then sat down beside him. "You shouldn't be sleeping out here you'll catch a cold you idiot!" The boy only groaned pulling away from her. "Isaac?...what's..." His face was still mostly hidden by the green hood, but she could make out the trail of tears staining his face. She shifted uncomfortably beside him playing with the stands of her cut off shorts. "Come on Lyna's is probably open by now I'll buy you some cookies." He said nothing. "I'll make sure to get Oatmeal this time."

He remained still and silent. "Isaac?" She reached out to pull him to face her; it felt so awkward to sit here with him like this. "Don't touch me!" He tossed his arm up slapping her hand away causing him to face her briefly; the coat slipped from around his shoulders and her heart nearly stopped by what she saw. "What on earth..." A small blue flower in a black pot rolled down his lap and onto the ground. Its roots stretched out from the tiny holes in the pot and appeared to be tethered to his wrist. Without the coat covering his back she could see that the flowers in the little garden had begun to grow up under his clothing; some were even sprouting from under his sleeve. "Isaac what did...?" She pulled him around to get a better look at him; panic stopped her breath as more of the flowers veined through his hood. Thousands of them spread across his face. They had shot out tiny tendrils that were burrowing under his skin. His eyes looked dull and lifeless. She pulled up his sleeves to find more of them had attached to his arms as well; the roots from the potted plant had burrowed deep into his main arteries. "Damn it you idiot!" She began tearing at the vines and roots ripping them from his skin. "What is wrong with you...you didn't have to do that if..." He did not resist her touch this time there was not enough strength in him if he had wanted to. "Come on!" She wedged her arm behind his back and under his legs then freed him from the flower's grasp. He was surprisingly light; his body went limp in her arms his head lulled against her chest as his eyes rolled to the back of his skull before drifting close. "Hang on Isaac!"

Dark curls slipped down her face as she leaned in to nibble on his ear. He reached up brushing the stray curl back with one ringed finger.

Knock Knock

"Ah Marky honey can't you just tell them to go away." Marco pushed the girl aside taking her hand in his and kissed it. "Sorry Angelina darling business comes first" …"ahh" a plumb violet tinted lip poked out in a mock pout and she stood up to answer the door. She pulled it open to a short bald man in a black blazer. "Sali, come in" Marco called from the sofa. The woman stepped aside letting him into the room she threw a reluctant look toward Marco before exiting then closed the door behind her. The man walked across the room and handed Marco a bottle of aspen blue water. "Graci, …So tell me Sali what brings you here today?" The short man eyed the door suspiciously. "Relax Sali she's a good girl feel free to speak" Marco leaned back tossing one arm over the back of the sofa and downed half the bottle of water before his short informant continued. "Sir, the Greek brothers are up to something" Marco waved it off, "So when aren't those fat meatballs up to no good eh" Salizar, or Sali as Marco fondly called him, pulled a chair up beside the sofa, and then motioned a request to sit. Marco nodded. Sali leaned in close, "I'm afraid they have one of ours helping them sir." Marco's dark brow shot up he was interested now, "do tell."

"Wait stop where are you going?' Sam attempted to keep up with the small bird as it wove through the trees deeper and deeper into the woods. The boy lay still in her arms only shifting or moaning slightly when the terrain got too rough. "Would you slow down you stupid bird!" She nearly fell over as Sedrick flew back at her full speed, stopping just an inch from her nose. Centering her eyes on the bird, she felt heat rise in her cheeks; a little ashamed for complaining. "Ok ok I get it I'll hurry" Sedrick took back off leading the way deeper in to where there were no paths. The noise from the city had faded a few hundred meters back there was nothing just the sounds of crows and the wind that disturbed the silence. Sam spared a glance every once in a while down to the boy sleeping in her arms too afraid to do more in fear she would lose track of her guide. *What is he? Is he like me?*, she wondered.

His face winced and he groaned. Breathing heavy, sweat glistened at his forehead. "Hang in there, I'll hurry just don't die on me I'm not about to owe you." She picked up her pace for a few more meters then stopped suddenly to the sound of rushing water. "A waterfall?"

The little bird landed in a tree at the edge of a glowing pool being fed by a rush of white mist. "What is a waterfall doing here?" A dark form distorted by the fall moved behind the rushing water. "Who's there?" Sedrick hopped off the branch and dove in after it. "Hey wait!" Sam laid Isaac down on the cool bank and ran toward the mist. The shadow drew closer and more solid until it emerged from the waterfall and took the shape of a large crane nearly as tall as Sam. It strolled across the pool taking no notice of her at first; it appeared focused on the boy lying on the ground. "NO don't" Sam ran around the pool waving her arms in an attempt to shoo the bird away. "Shoo get away what are you doing?" The bird backed away as Sam approached still waving her arms; it turned its long bill toward the girl seemingly noticing her for the first time. "So you are the one" "What...it talks?"... The long pointed bill dipped down in a low bow "Forgive me"

Sam dropped down beside Isaac and snatched him from the ground holding him protectively in her lap. "Just what are you and what were you going to do to Isaac?"

The bird stepped toward the bank. "Please allow me to introduce myself..." The advancement only caused the girl to pull the boy closer. "Get away from him!" Surprised the bird stepped back stretching up to its full height which was easily a few inches taller than Sam. It looked from side to side blinking wildly. It suddenly seemed uncertain of its surroundings then it spread its wings and flew away.

"Hey...what the hell kind of introduction was that?" A sharp pain to the top of her head followed the leave of the large crane. "Ouww!" She reached up rubbing the top of her head where Sedrick had pecked her smartly then flew up into a tree branch fanning its tail feathers at her. "And where the hell did you go?" she scolded while shaking her fist at the bird....The soft sound of Isaac's breath brought her attention back to her lap..."ngh"..."Isaac?" She rested a cool palm upon his forehead. Brushing aside a few stray bits of remaining plant matter, she bent down placing her forehead to his. His skin burned beneath hers. "What am I supposed to do... I knew I should have just taken you to the hospital instead of following that stupid bird" Something wet drop onto Sam's scalp; clenching her fist, she grumbled, "You had better not have shit on me Sedrick or I swear I'll cook you"..."Well now that would teach him" the voice was smooth as it floated down to her. "Who?" She lifted her head up to lock eyes with a form looming above her. It appeared to be made entirely of water, with two floating blue jewels set where its eyes should be. "AHHH!..." Sam nearly fell backward taking Isaac with her. She didn't believe it; if she hadn't seen it herself and hadn't pinched herself so hard she nearly cried she wouldn't have. Hovering just above the pool was the torso of a beautiful man made entirely of liquid. "Sorry about my previous guise it takes so much energy to keep this form. It is just easier to possess an animal...isn't that right Lum?" His shining blue eyes turned toward the small blue bird. Sedrick in turn picked a berry out of the tree and tossed it at the water. The berry passed through his torso and out the other side; he shook his head with a sigh. "As sensitive as always I see"

Sam pulled Isaac's body a little closer and started inching away from the water. "Um excuse me, but I came here to help Isaac; can you help him or not?" The water sprite turned his attention back to the girl "Forgive me I haven't seen my old friend in decades..." He turned his shining gaze up toward the tree "... it wouldn't kill you to come visit Lum..." He then turned back toward the girl on the bank "...I digress, my name is

Renlacir guardian of beast and king of the water sprites and what might your name be?" Sam backed away nervously, "Um its Samantha...Sam for short... and you have got to be a hallucination" Icy lids closed over his brilliant gaze. For a moment Sam felt a wave of relief as the light shining from the water vanished. He appeared upset. "I see" Renlacir bowed his head and his body began to melt back into the water until he vanished as a mere ripple across the surface. "Hey...I thought you were supposed to help me!" she shouted as the last ripple dissipated... "Not that I could get help from a hallucination anyway. I really should stop spending so much time growing those plants" she grumbled...."nngg" Sam pulled her eyes from the water and rested her hand on Isaac's forehead, he was still burning up. "I guess I'll just have to carry you back into the city..." she looked around and frowned "...that is if I could find my way back" Her caramel pools drifted back down to the boy in her arms. "What am I supposed to do now?" she sighed. She pressed an ear to his chest. His heart beat was faint, but steady. She closed her eyes allowing the rhythm of his heart to lull her. It was funny the more she listened to it the more it started to sound like the lapping of water. It grew louder and louder until it roared like the ocean. Her eyes shot open to a wall of water rising above the trees; then it came crashing down upon her sweeping Isaac out of her arms and into the pool. "ISAAC!"

A.J. Zanders

Ch. 12

"Isaac!" Sam stared at the rushing water debating if the plunge was worth it. "You stupid water sprite come back here with Isaac, I don't know how to swim!" she shouted into the receding waves. The water sprite did not answer. The water quieted and she could feel the mist of the waterfall again. It was apparent Isaac wasn't coming back. "Damn it! You owe me big for this Isaac!" Sam threw her shoes on the bank, took a deep breathe, and dove in after him.

The instant she hit the icy water, her breath left her body. She struggled to get it back. Her blood rushed back to her heart as her body tried to preserve her core temperature, leaving her limps lifeless pieces of wood. Slapping at the frigid liquid, she was whisked back toward the waterfall and into the cave behind it. It took every bit of her strength just to keep her head above the water. She traveled for over half a mile from the waterfall her legs swished behind her like logs and the freezing temperatures were already starting to make her sleepy. There was no strength left, she was ready to give in; maybe it would be nice to let the icy folds cradle her until she fell asleep to rest on the bottom of the stream. Her eyes closed without reservation she didn't want to fight it anymore. But she didn't have to struggle for much longer; the spring dumped her into a pool at the back of the cavern. For a moment she was allowed to fill her lungs with precious air. She gulped at the cool air greedily until she drifted to the center of the pool. A sense of Peace washed over her, she had been saved; and then something tugged at her ankle. This might have served as a warning if it had not been for the numbness in her limbs. It wasn't until it yanked her under that she realized that she had been tossed from the frying pan and into the fire. She felt the crushing icy water push the air from her lungs like a tube of toothpaste. She watched helplessly as the milky surface rose above her lids. *After all of that, this is it huh? I guess I should have learned how to swim? Sorry Isaac*

"SAM!... Sam are you here?" Lewie banged urgently on the wooden door. "Sam it's me Lewie please open up!" He pressed his ear to the door and sighed. "I really didn't want to have to do this" He kicked at the decrypted door as hard as he could. The wood around the lock cracked then shattered. "Alright once more should do it" The brass broke free with one more hard strike from Lewie's foot. The door swung open into the empty room. It looked as if a wild boar had been trapped inside. His eyes traveled along the discarded bed-sheets, then over to the table where the watering can lay on its side leaking on the ground, then up to the back door perched open. *Don't tell me they...?* Lewie spun on his heels and out of Sam's apartment. There were only two places he could think they would take her and neither was good.

Sam felt the current shift and the pull of the undertow reversed and tossed her up onto the bank. She drug herself up letting her diaphragm push the water from her lungs then flopped over on to her back to stare up into leering bright blue-green eyes. It was painful just to breath; it was so dark the only light seemed to be coming from the boy's eyes sockets. She winced at the brightness then her lids refused to open again. His name left her lips as the overwhelming urge to sleep took hold of her. "Isaac?" Sam welcomed the sleep that pulled at her and allowed her mind to drift off though the darkness.

A few hours later Sam regained consciousness. She was no longer frozen instead she was wrapped in something warm and fuzzy; it covered all, but her head and it smelt like dirt and moss. *What a crappy dream.* She heard the familiar sound of water dripping echoing off the walls; *stupid leaky basement...wait a minute.* Her eyes shot open, but her body refused to move. Her entire body felt as heavy and immobile as a wet quilt. "nng..where am I?" She let her head fall to the side to find the boy lying beside her. "Isaac?"....."But how I thought...?" A scratchy voice echoed off the walls. "That's a water sprite for you" Sam struggled to lift her head toward the sound. "Who's there?" An old woman with a blue handkerchief tied around unruly gray and purple hair sat hunched over a fire. She pulled a gourd from her side and tipped it's contains onto the fire. It roared into a bright blaze, sending grotesque shadows across her craggy face.

Sam flinched at the intense heat and light. Pushing herself off the ground, the woman stood up, then shuffled toward Sam with an arm load of wrinkled items. As the woman stepped closer Sam could see a pointed nose poking out past the blue kerchief. There were dark charred marks adorning her old withered face. "It's you." The old woman didn't respond she just nudged the furry blanket with her foot. It moved with a groan and she dropped the bundle of clothing on top of Sam. "Here"

Pushing herself up, Sam watched a large bear stroll across the cave. "What the..." Her eye shot back toward the woman, "is that a bear?" Wisteria set down a large canvas bag and began digging through its contents; completely ignoring the girl's question. "Excuse me are even listening to me?" Wisteria didn't even look up. "You're not blind child what do you think it is?" Sam couldn't believe this woman. "You let a bear sleep on me?"..."Ka ha ha... you should be thanking that bear...he's the reason you didn't lose all your toes last night" Wisteria continued to sort through jars and pouches until she found what she was looking for. She held up a brown package wrapped in a twine. "Here we are" She pulled the string and peeled back the folds. Inside was a red powder. She poured some clear rancid liquid into the center and stirred it with a stick. The smell burned Sam's eyes. *cough* "What is that stuff?" Wisteria regarded her briefly, "Its capsaicin it will help bring heat back to his skin" She turned back to Isaac and pulled the covers from his body; his skin was bluish. His narrow chest rose and fell as he took ragged breaths. Fear pulled at Sam's heart. "Is he going to be ok?" The old woman was done answering the girl's incessant questions and set to work on Isaac. Sam released a frustrated sigh "Fine I'll just check for myself…" Sam stopped dead as the woman pulled the blankets completely off the boy, not a scrap of clothing covered him. Heat rose into Sam's cheeks in a brilliant red and she quickly turned around. "Jeez give the kid some privacy" Sam chastised the woman. A dry laugh, something between a cough and a chuckle, puffed from the woman's lips. "Well you were the one looking….Besides, I've cared for this boy ever since he was a baby he ain't got nothing I've never seen before." She rubbed the red goop between her hands and started smearing it all over Isaac's body. His chest rose in a heavy breath, then his body jolted as he coughed from the fumes, but he did not wake. Soon he settled down peacefully and Wisteria covered him with fresh blankets. Still uncertain if it was safe to look Sam continued to stare down at the bundle of clothing in her arms. "So you must be his Aunt Wisteria" she sputtered through the embarrassment. "Well I sure ain't his mother" Her amber eyes drifted down to the boy now bundled in several blankets. Wisteria stared down at him for a few moments then pushed herself up in a salvo of creaks and pops. "Damn old age" She muttered. Sam turned around and scooted up closer to get a better look at the boy. He appeared so serene now. The bits of plants had all been washed away and the wounds they had left behind were just a memory, the color of his cheeks had returned and he was sleeping peacefully now. She felt a shiver run up her spine. Her entire body was freezing. "Here." She felt something warm and heavy drape over her shoulders and she pulled it in close. She looked over her shoulder to the old woman and muttered her thanks. Her gaze dropped back down to the boy's sleeping face. "What is he?" she asked attentively, uncertain if this was a question she would have answered. "He's a sprite." Wisteria said matter of factly. Sam shivered slightly under the old woman's shawl. "A sprite huh?" The old woman looked the girl over; a frown tugged at her lips "You should change too", she said indicating the bundle in the girl's arms. Sam looked down to the assortment of clothing. "Oh yeah I guess I should" She held it at arm's length and shook out the wrinkles. It was an old grey dress with long sleeves and a waistcoat; copper buttons and everything. "Jeez when were these things made, oh well at least they're dry" Sam glanced over to the boy still sleeping; even so she wasn't really comfortable changing in the same room with him. Noticing a small crevice at the back of the cave, Sam carried the change of clothes over to it. It looked large enough to change in.

Sam pulled the shawl from her shoulders and stuffed it up into tiny fissures. It served as a makeshift curtain. She stripped the wet clothes from her body and stepped into the old fashion dress. She had to fight with the buttons higher up her back. As she struggled two voices rang throughout the cave. She froze. *Why am so I nervous they know I'm here.* "Why did you bring her here... she's human she shouldn't be here" came a raspy voice. "I did not bring her here she followed me on her own, and you and I both know she isn't just a human" responded a smooth voice Sam assumed was Renlacir. The curiosity was too much she hooked a finger around the edge of the 'curtain' pulling it back to peek around the fuzzy wool. She could make out two shadows moving along the walls; one was obviously the grumpy old woman the other she couldn't really make out. All she saw were a few gestures as the other shadow seemed to be pointing in her direction. Then the shadows parted and one of the voices came in her direction followed by a few light footsteps. "Samantha are you decent?" Sam tossed the curtain back over the opening with an 'eep'. Ren's footsteps faltered. "Is that a 'no'"...Sam rushed to fasten the buttons. "Um no I mean yes I mean just a minute" she said in a shaky voice. When she pulled back the shawl; two bright blue eyes blinked out at her. She was so startled by

what she saw she nearly fell back into the crevice.
He looks just like Isaac!

"Who...are you?" He flashed a wide impish
smile past his wet limp seaweed-like bangs "Have
you forgotten me already Samantha...well let me
reintroduce myself" ..."Renlacir at your service"
he said while making a low bow. He took her
hand in his and placed his forehead to its smooth
back. His brow was cold and wet. She jerked it
back in alarm. A thin blue brow shot up in
response to her reaction. "I'm sorry I did not mean
to come on so strong" Sam stepped back shaking
her head as she tried to stifle a giggle. She couldn't
help it; he looked completely ridiculous. He was
wearing an oversized brown blazer with plaid
orange and brown pants that were obviously
made for a man well over six feet. His royal
countenance twisted into mild curiosity, "What on
earth is so funny?" ..."Your clothes..." she said
pointing to his chosen outfit. He pulled himself up
right to his fullest height and attempted to look as
regal as possible which only caused a deeper
giggle and a snort from his audience. "Ooo...k ok
ha ha ha...stop already pftt ha ha" The sprite king
was not amused. "You laugh at royalty, have you

looked at yourself young lady?" he said with a little pout. He reached out grabbing her wrist to pull her toward the edge of the pool. Sam quickly pulled the shawl from the rock to cover her exposed back.

As they stepped up to the pool Renlacir waved his arm over the surface clearing the milky liquid away to reveal crystal clear water. "There you see we are twins we both look ridiculous." he said with a huge grin pulling at his pale face. He really did look just like Isaac especially when he smiled. Sam stared down at her puffy bleached blonde and green hair, the demur grey dress, and the ratty wool shawl slipping from her shoulders. It all made her look like a schoolmarm on her last nerve. She stepped back from the pool her hands working fervently to smooth out her unruly hair. "Damn it I hate this hair" After desperately trying to tame her wild mane without much luck she bowed slightly to the water sprite king in apology. "I'm sorry I shouldn't have laughed at you; it was just that your attire didn't exactly match your um... status" Renlacir blinked back at her in curiosity. "Status?... Oh the whole king thing well, I can't say I really have status anymore. Most of the water sprites are gone." His cheerful expression fell into a despondent frown. He stepped away from the pool as if his own reflection saddened him. He suddenly looked frail and worn. "There aren't enough of us left to worry about that and most of the wood sprites are currently residing as trees. What good is a king to a tree?"

The sprite lord, drug the oversized pants with him as he shuffled over to the boy resting by the pool. Sam watched him drag the hem of the pants along the ground hiking them up every so often so as not to trip on them. She told herself as she watched him cross the rocky surface that she would have to apologize to Lewie; that really was pretty funny.

Renlacir gathered up his loose clothing and knelt down by Isaac; he pushed up an oversized sleeve and brushed a strand of hair from the boy's forehead. With the two of them so close it was more obvious than ever that these two were related somehow. Sam walked over, gathering her unsecured dress so as not to trip on it or have it fall off, then settled in next to the water sprite. "So tell me just who are you?" Renlacir looked up from the boy blinking innocently at the girl. "Did you forget again?" Sam waved her hand in front of her face, "No I don't mean your name I mean who are you to Isaac you two look almost identical."

Ren's face lit up and beamed with pride the wide impish smile returned to the corners of his mouth. "I was really hoping he would get some of my good looks" ... "What!" she said a little surprised.

"Isaac as you call him, is my son after all; I thought it was pretty obvious" He looked back down resting his hand on the boy's forehead. "Good his fever has gone down" So he was going to be ok and he wasn't an orphan after all. Somehow the thought made Sam feel a little out of place. She let her eyes drift around the walls of the cavern. "Lord Renlacir, Where are we?" The water sprite looked up from the boy and over to the girl still gazing about the hollows of the cave. "You could just call me Ren. ...Renlacir sounds so umm what is the word I'm looking for...up..id..tee" Sam smiled, "Ok Lord Ren where is this place" He frowned a little at her insistent use of the word 'Lord'. "We are on the border of the water sprite kingdom and the wood sprite kingdom or at least that is what it used to be...now I'd say we are in a cave behind a waterfall...doesn't sound as impressive does it?" He turned from the girl to call over to his longtime friend. "Isn't that right Koda?" The bear was playing with a stick floating in the pool. "Rooarr" was the bear's response before he went back to playing with his new found toy. Ren then turned back to Sam and flashed her one of his toothy grins. It was difficult for Sam to believe that this childish individual could be any sort of king. She looked down to Isaac and then over to Renlacir he seemed to look a little sad every time he gazed down onto his son. "Samantha, would you look after him for me?"... "What! Me? Why?"

Ren's eye's never left his son, "because he needs someone he can relate to, someone he feels he can trust. I felt it there; didn't you, he loves you?"... "What! But I hardly know him" Ren tucked the blankets around his son ignoring Sam's protest. "He's very special Sam, as are you. The two of you need each other. My sister told me of his fate long before he was even born. I wish I knew of a way to prevent it. Maybe you can be the key to saving him." Sam looked up at the sprite king confusion and disbelief settled on her features. "Wait what fate?" Ren ignored her question and stood up to walk over to the bear now swimming in the pool. *Ok maybe a less uncomfortable question* Sam thought. "Um Lord Ren…"…"Just *Ren* is fine Samantha." The use of her full name irritated her so she got the point. "Oh sorry…Ren does Isaac know…that you are his father?" The water sprite just shook his head; the frown pulling at his lips, only pulled harder. Ok obviously not a more comfortable question. "Well now's your chance to tell him. Yeah, why not, he thinks he's an orphan…his mother died right? Well don't you think he would be happy to know his father is alive?" Sam tried to cheer him up, but was curtly interrupted by a harsh and blunt "No!"… "It would be best for Isaac not to know a coward like him is his father." The raspy voice ridiculed from the cave entrance. Both heads turned toward the mouth of the cave to where the old sprite stood with a long pipe between her teeth, a small blue bird perched on her shoulder. "Wisteria?" Sam watched the pain of her words fill the water sprite's eyes. She turned and snapped at the old woman. "What the hell!

Just because you're bitter and alone doesn't mean Isaac has to be too!" The old woman's amber eyes drift over to the girl in a deep scowl. "Shut it girlie you have known him what a day a week maybe; I've raised that boy from the moment he took his first breath don't tell me you know what that boy wants" …"Nggh"

Three sets of eyes shot toward Isaac as he shifted in his sleep. The boy took a deep breath rolled over on his side then settled back down. There was tension between all three as they wondered if the boy had heard anything they had said. It was Wisteria who broke the silence, "Girl I think it is time you go home…I'll lead you back to the park…come." She turned away heading for the exit leaving no room to argue. Sam looked down at Isaac reluctant to leave his side. Renlacir seemed to sense this and patted her lightly on the shoulder. "I'll keep watch over him he will be fine I'm sure your family is worried about you"… "uh…yeah sure" Sam looked away a little too ashamed to admit she didn't have a family to go home to. It would just sound like she was trying to get pity. She stood up to follow the old woman. She stopped to look back at the boy and the sprite king knelling beside him. Ren flashed a reassuring smile and she turned away, disappearing from the cave with the old woman. Once outside the large cavern Wisteria stopped. Sam nearly ran into her. "Hold it a second girlie" Sam was shocked as Wisteria reached up pulling the shawl from the girl's shoulders. The cool cave air set goose bump racing up Sam's bare back. "Hey wait…I wasn't going to keep it, but I need it right now."…"Hush! Now turn around!" Sam reluctantly turned her back to the old sprite. Wisteria draped the wool cover across her shoulder then set to work at the task at hand. The girl was tall and slender. The grey dress was fit all the way to her neck, it was no wonder she couldn't fasten the last few buttons. Wisteria reached up to the first loose copper button and began working her way up. As her stiff and calloused fingers worked the buttons they brushed along soft welts along the girl's back. Her hands froze. *I'm sorry child if I had known.* Wisteria's head fell and she took a deep breath before fastening the last button. She pulled the shawl from her shoulder and placed it around the girl's. "There…you shouldn't show so much skin it can get you into trouble" Sam pulled the shawl close and turned to face the old woman, "Thank you."…"Whatever lets go." Wisteria turned back toward the exit and continued out expecting the girl to follow. For just a moment Sam thought there was a kind yet just a little shy heart in the old woman and began to wonder if she might allow her to see Isaac again. "Forget it girl…there is no need for you to return to this place and its best for all of us if you just forget everything you saw today!" Sam stared at the woman's frizzy hair sticking out of the back of her kerchief in shock. *How did she? Well so much for a shy kind heart.* A faint light filled the end of the cave. The woods were filled with the moon's light as they emerged, she could still hear the rush of water. They must have exited from another opening, to the cave, somewhere behind the waterfall. Sam's heart sank as the sound of rushing water faded into the background of the forest. "You know it isn't fair to Isaac. All he's had all his life is you to look after him, because you wouldn't tell him about his father." The old woman didn't flitch she continue to press on through the woods. "Listen I'm free to come to the park whenever I want so if Isaac comes out to see me there really isn't anything you could do about it" Wisteria stopped and spun around on her heels. "You listen girlie you don't know a thing about that boy…he's more complex then you could imagine. He's not just some sniffling kid who needs a father to play catch with. He's the blood of this forest and he needs to understand that. This forest is made up of sprites not just trees and that boy is the only one who can free them. I don't need him distracted by a girl or his deadbeat father. So zip it when you don't know what you're talking about!" Wisteria turned back around in a silent command that the girl should continue following her without another word. Sam knew this battle was over; one point old hag, Sam zero, but she would get hers next time.

The lamp cast its light along the ground and over to a thick white oak. A man in a heavy blazer was hidden in its shadow. He cracked his hairy knuckles and nodded to another figure hidden behind another tree a few meters away. Each one nodded to the next until all six men were aware of the girl's approach. Sam stepped out of the darkness glancing back as the old woman's footsteps faded. "I wonder if I'll ever get to see him again." Her shoulders fell, as the sinking feeling the answer to that question was 'no'. A wave of sadness settled in her stomach. She was sure that the old woman would interfere as much as possible from now on. It was very unlikely that she would be able to get close to Isaac again. *Well he has his father now…why would he want to come back into my world anyway?* The trees thinned; her mind drifted back toward the cave and the sleeping boy, Sam was completely unaware of the danger waiting for her under the lamp light. She winced at the city lights as they hit her eyes the instant she stepped out into the park. She closed her lids for just a second to adjust back to the city's harsh brightness; it was one second too long. Her lashes shot opened as she felt something rough and cold press against her nose and mouth. A thick sweetness penetrated her nostrils sending a buzz of dizziness swirling around in her head. She wanted to pull away, to kick, to scream anything, but her head felt light and her body heavy; she went limp against a broad sturdy chest. Massive arms kept her from hitting the ground.

Ch. 13

*"A young woman will
free our savior"*

The fire sent eerie shadow's dancing along the cavern walls. Wisteria poked at the glowing logs and sneezed. "Damn damp cavern…only fit for a worthless water imp." Ren shifted uncomfortably near the pool "I see you're still angry" Wisteria pulled her dull ambers from the fire and set them adrift across the cavern toward the milky water where the sprite king sat along its edge his legs submersed to his knees. "You should not have brought her here; I never wanted her to know." Ren ignored the old woman's banter and continued to silently stroke the bear's ears. Koda had made himself comfortable next to the water sprite and rested his head peacefully in Ren's lap. Feeling, Wisteria's burning glare, Ren gently laid the bear's head aside and pulled his feet from the pool. He walked somberly over to his son, then settle down next to him. Wisteria noted he was keeping his distance from her and the fire. "Why so far away does fire still frighten you… afraid you'll evaporate …ka ha ka ha." He shot her a cool glance. "Well, it isn't like a wood sprite to get along so well with fire either." as soon as the words left his lips he regretted it. The woman's face twisted from a sneer to hurt. "Shut it you damn guppy… if it weren't for me you would never have even seen your precious son again." Ren bowed his head a little ashamed of himself he knew what Wisteria had done and what it had cost her. "I apologize, Wisteria that was uncalled for. If I could give it back to you I would." Wisty snorted "Some king." she turned back to poking the fire. She wasn't the only one who'd suffered that past few centuries. "Oh stuff it…you leak enough as it is" Ren smiled he knew that was as good of an exoneration he was going to get from the old wood sprite. He reached out smoothing the wild hairs of the boy sleeping so peacefully. "If only there were a way…I'd take his place." He stared down at the boy's soft features that so resembled his mother's. "Wisteria…how did she die?

The first thing Sam felt was the cold stone pressing against her shoulder as she fought to pry her eyes open, but they felt so heavy almost like they were glued together. She tried to reach up to wipe away whatever was keeping her eyes shut, but found she couldn't move her arms. The closer she got to wakefulness the stronger the pounding in her head became. "Ngh"....

"Well, well it looks like our sleeping beauty is finally awake." Sam managed to shift her weight up against something tall and solid and leaned back turning her head toward the voice. She still couldn't open her eyes, but the strong smell of cigar smoke mixed with brute aftershave told her everything she needed to know. "I'd know that raunchy smell anywhere...Jimmy Greek" She heard a light snort followed by another's voice. "Still sassy even all tied up...I'm impressed my Chicka" Sam forgot the ache in her body as the shock washed over her. "Marco?" Marco stepped a little closer "I must say that is not a good look for you Sammie." She could hear his chilling snicker. She felt so foolish she could only point her head the direction she thought Marco was in and shouted at him. "Stuff it Asshole...why are you working with these Fat Grecians anyway you traitor!"

She heard his weight shift and his voice rise slightly then lowered to a snide cueing. "Traitor you say...ah now I am hurt Sammie, besides it doesn't really matter now does it, but if there is a

traitor it's your precious Lewie...aw what's that
look for you didn't think I knew."

Sam felt a breath hot and rancid and she tried to
turn her head away, but was quickly stopped by a
wide callused palm. A twisted smile pulled at
Johnny's lips as he pulled her face up in the
direction of the greased Sicilian sitting across from
her his legs crossed leaning back in his velvet
winged chair looking royal. "Here is the deal
Sammie you bring me that little miracle worker
you've been seeing and I let you and Lewie live."

The effects of the drug they had use to knock her
out was fully starting to wear off and her eye lids
loosened allowing her to peek past blonde lashes
toward Marco leaning forward; his chin resting on
his folded hands.

"What are you talking about?"
The Sicilian wagged a finger at her "Tsk, tsk, you
shouldn't lie Chicka" Marco pushed himself up
and over to her hunched form then lowered
himself to her eye-level. She could smell the grease
slicking back his hair.

"Don't play dumb...it doesn't suit you...much
like that outfit your wearing."..."Lewie thought
he was being so smart offering you to the Greek

brothers if they promised to treat you better than me, Now Sammie I wasn't that awful was I?" Sam scowled at him. "Well thanks to Lewie's bit of information I've made them a better offer."

Lewie you idiot.

Marco reached out snatching her face from Johnny's "Now listen unless you want me to mess up this pretty face of yours you'll do as I say…" Sam challenged his glare with one of her own. "Just kill me already…I'm tired of being your damn puppet." she wrenched her face free and spat in his face. "ugh" Marco wiped the spittle from his face an evil twisted grin pulled at his lips causing the dimple in his chin to bore deeper, "Now that isn't very lady like Sammie girl…" His hand shot back out wrapping around her mouth so firm she couldn't open it; she could barely breathe. "I'm afraid it doesn't work that way if you are dead I can't get my hands on that little golden goose, in the forest, now can I and besides I can't promise Lewie won't get caught up in some gang dispute and get himself killed…but if that is what you want." Sam pulled her eyes away sick of looking into his sneering face. "Ok fine … just…leave him out of this." Marco patted the girl's cheek. "Good girl." He gestured for Johnny to release her. She felt her body fall forward and felt the crack as her skull met the pavement unable to catch herself. Sam glared up through hazy eyes from the cold concrete floor. Three of them stood leering at her as the urge to sleep pulled at her lids. "I'll get even with you bastards" she was the only one to hear her threat as the walls faded and everything went dark.

A.J. Zanders

Ch. 14

"A bond will be formed"

"Lum!...Lum where are you?" Renlacir glided along the river as the fires continued to consume the forest. "LUUUMMM!" ..."Damn that girl why did she go off on her own like that?" The river twisted through the forest toward the wood sprite's kingdom. He just knew his foolish sister would try to rescue that boy on her own. "Lum answer me already!" His azure eyes scanned through the smoke until he saw a tiny figure *laying on the ground curled protectively around something. "LUM!" He focused all his energy until his body was in a solid form then pulled it from the river. He raced across the smoking ground the sound of water sizzled with each step. "LUM!" He knelt down next to his sister; in her embrace was a nest. Two baby birds just out of their shell their mouths a gap and their little heads lulled over the edge. "Oh Lum"…"wait…what's this?" Under the two small bodies was a tiny speckled egg. "This one hasn't hatched yet, maybe…" He gently wrapped his hand around the tiny egg; he could still feel its heartbeat. "Ren? Is that you *cough*"…"Lum?"… "Ngh…Ren? ….I'm sorry I didn't listen to you…I… couldn't…stop them…*cough* *cough*….please take care of him…" Ren looked down into his palm then back to his sister as her eyes closed and her breathing became shallow. Steam rose from her body and her flesh started to disintegrate. "Lum…you foolish girl!" He too could start to feel the effects of the smoke and intense heat. His body wouldn't last much longer. He had to get back to the river. He rested his hand on his sister's forehead whispering something in her ear. Her body began to dissolve until all that was left was a small blue jewel which he cupped tenderly in his hand then took both the jewel and the tiny egg back to the river.*

"I'm sorry Lum" Milky tears ran down his pale face as the memory faded. Deep blue eyes opened to stare past silver lashes up at the rocky ceiling. His head spun around the nightmare he hadn't had in centuries. "Ugh I forgot dreams were a down side to having a solid form like this." He reached up cupping his forehead with a cool damp hand, and then focused on the small bundle curled up under the blankets beside him and frowned. Wisteria's voice broke his trance. "It is thanks to you he is better…at least you can say that" Ren looked up from the boy to the old sprite still huddled by the small fire. A thin smile pulled at his blue lips. The old woman had a heart after all. "Ngh…" Two sets of eyes shot toward the boy as he shifted then rolled over on to his back his hand went up to cradle his forehead. "Where?" Isaac's eyes shot open to the sound of a splash and pushed himself up to investigate; his eyes settled on a hunched form by the fire. "Wisty…where am I…how did?" He looked down at his attire and around the cave once more. "What happened I don't really remember…my head hurt, there were so many screams…I…can't…"

A.J. Zanders

Wisteria stood up wrapping the blanket around
the boy's shoulders and led him over to the fire. "I
think it is time you understood your position
Porty...come sit." Isaac looked back at the pool of
milky water moving in small short waves then
turned back to Wisteria. "Wisty,...why do you call
me Porty?" The old woman shook her head and
laughed. "I called you that many years ago when
your mother was still alive. We are not allowed to
name our children it is up to Gurrell, that stump of
ash you met the other day" She grumbled while
tossing another log on the fire. "I was just a girl
when you were born... I always hated the name
that damn tree gave me...when I saw you bundled
up in your mother's arms your hair all sticking up
I immediately thought about my sister's
pet...anyway since you were never given a name I
decided to call you Porty. Now, enough of that,
come sit" Wisteria patted the ground beside her.
Isaac walked over staring at the fire then settled
down opposite. Wisteria released a sigh and shook
her head then began her tale. Isaac sat silently as
she relayed three centuries of history from the
moment his mother was chosen to the time he was
resurrected from the guardian tree Gurrell. His

204

face scrunched into a thoughtful scowl. "NO! I don't believe it...why would humans do that...How can I be here if I was sealed inside a tree...you're just making it up so I'll hate humans like you do!" Isaac tossed the blanket to the ground and stood to leave. "Wait son...please she isn't lying!"

Isaac stopped and turned toward the sound of the new voice coming from within the echo of dripping water. His eyes narrowed at the wavering milky surface. There was no one there; had he imagined he heard someone...no. Something pushed through and stood about three feet above the surface. Isaac rubbed his eyes and stepped a little closer. Hovering above the water was a torso and the head of a man made entirely of water. The figure gave him a nervous smile and spoke again. "Hello son,...or should I just call you Isaac?" Isaac fell back smacking his tail bone onto the rough rocky floor. "Uh...maybe I should have waited..." Ren laughed nervously.

Isaac shot a look toward Wisteria hoping for answers. The old woman just shrugged and stood up to walk away leaving Isaac alone with the strange new being. "It is nice to finally meet you...well while you're awake anyway." Isaac stared back up into the gleaming blue lights of the figures eyes. "I see you are speechless well, I guess it is better than being threatened and insulted the way your friend greeted me." Ren's eyes traveled around the cave then stopped to rest on his bewildered son who looked much like a fish gasping for the comfort of the river. Isaac just couldn't find his voice was there really some being made of water capable of talking floating in front of him, or was he still dreaming?

Ren's head fell and his body melted back into the pool only to reemerge on the bank in an oversized dripping wet brownish suit. "Is this better?" he gave the boy another weary smile. This was just more Isaac couldn't seem to handle and he backed away. A small blue bird dove between Isaac and the man currently dripping on the cave floor. "Sederick?", "Lum?"

The little bird hopped over to Isaac's outstretched hand and bowed slightly then flew over to the man in the soaked crumbled brown suit. Ren reached up patting the small bird on the head. "Thank you Lum" He then turned his attention to Isaac. "Let me introduce you...Isaac this is my sister, ahem your aunt Lum…you have been calling her Sederick I believe." Lum spread a wing out and bowed "Lum? …Aunt?" Isaac blinked back the confusion. "Wait you're a girl?"

Sam sat up rubbing her sore head. "I need to stop making a habit of this." Her blurry vision cleared as her eyes traveled the room. She was back in her apartment, but everything was gone: her plants, all her supplies even some of her personal items were gone. The room was completely striped except a piece of paper stuck to the door. "What the hell?" Sam swung her legs around to set her feet on the cold concrete. She quickly picked them back up as the icy floor stung her feet. "Damn its cold" She pulled a blanket from her bed; the only thing left in her room, around her body and made her way to the door pulling the note from it.

- My Chicka-

We have someone very precious to you. I'll give you a hint his name starts with an "L". I can't guarantee his safety, the Greek brothers are pretty pissed that he left them out of such a sweet deal ie... that little jewel of yours. So let's trade shall we? You bring me the little golden goose and I give you back your precious brother.

-Ciao-

"How the hell did he know?" Sam crumbled the letter and threw it. "That bastard! of all the low..." her steam quickly dissipated as her anger turned to despair. "What am I supposed to do now?"

Ch. 15

"A trust will be broken"

Isaac sat cross legged staring up the base of a massive burnt fossil of a tree as the sun slowly rose to warm his back. "So it's true…what I saw" he spoke more to himself then the tree. Lum landed beside him and lowered her head. "And you what should I call you Lum…Sederick…Auntie…" It was the first time she had ever heard anger in the boy's voice it went beyond hurt and sorrow; he was furious. "Is that all I am good for...is that the only reason she cared for me?" An iridescent tear trickled down his cheek as he continued to stare at the burnt bark. "I'm just a sacrifice for people I've never met and no one remembers." He shoved his hands in his pockets. Something small and flat, slightly square rattled amongst the soft cotton. "What's this?" He pulled the small object from his pocket. It was a small red and white box, on the top was a picture of a cowboy on a bucking bronco. He pushed his finger into the small box sliding it open and frowned. There were two matches left rolling around the near empty box. He closed the box shaking it near his ear like a baby with a rattle, then turned to look down at the small blue bird. "How about it Auntie Lum...I could just set this entire forest on fire and there wouldn't be anyone left to save" Images flashed before the bird's dark orbs. It was a vision she hoped she'd never have to witness with her own two eyes. She leaped up in panic diving for the small white box, but he quickly snatched the matches from her grasp and shoved them back inside his pocket. "Don't worry

I haven't decided yet…tell Wisteria I won't be
back for a while and don't follow me …Sederick"
he bit out the name as if severing any ties he had
ever had with the bird. He didn't even glance back
as he walked away leaving Lum to stand in the
center of a graveyard of trees. She shook her tiny
head as she watched the boy disappear into the
forest. She could still remember so vividly the
same defiance of a certain woman with long
flowing chestnut hair.

*The silver moon dance along the surface of the
rippling water as it washed up on the bank. "Lumeria?
Are you here?" Rowan stepped into the cool water and
scanned its depth. "Princess Lumeria I need to speak
with you."*

*Two spheres of light shot out from the reflection of the
moon and raced toward the shore. Within seconds they
forced the water up into a narrow dome then contorted
and twisted until it took the shape of a girl. "Yes
Priestess I am here why do you call me?" Rowan
sighed. Lumeria was just a girl after all, she couldn't
take her frustrations out on her. The girl was only
telling the wood sprites what she saw. "Lum I need to
know of another way…surly you must know of a way
to save my son." Lum looked away. It wasn't like she*

*wanted the prince to die, and she had attempted
revisiting the vision, but nothing was ever different.
"I'm sorry Priestess I understand you were forced into
having that child. Then fell in love with him, just to
have him ripped from your arms in the future. I truly
am sorry, but I do not see any other way to save your
village." Lum truly wished there were a way to comfort
the priestess, but Rowan would never have accepted it
anyway. "That is not why I had the boy; I do not care
what happens to that village. If you know a way I may
change his fate then tell me." Lum averted her gaze. She
knew of a way, but it was forbidden. It would require
someone else taking his place and even with that there
was no guarantee it would work. "There is a way, but it
means more suffering for the one to take his place and
I'm not even sure it would work." Rowan knelt down
level with the water sprite child. "Please Lum don't you
want to save him?" Lum timidly leaned in close to the
woman's ear, "To save the forest the blood of water and
the blood of wood must join…inside one body. I tell you
this because I love the prince too…that union does not
have to be a baby…" Lum moved away and
concentrated on a solid form. Once she was complete
opaque; she traced her fingertips along the water's
surface. It instantly turned to ice at her touch. She
smashed it with her fist and picked up a jagged shard*

then pierced her wrist. A silver like liquid dribbled from her arm. She gathered it into a small blue vile and handed it to Rowan. "I'm sorry this is all I can do for you, it is up to you if it is worth the sacrifice." Rowan reached out taking the vile and tied a piece of her long hair though a small hole in the neck and slipped it over her head. Lum watched with sad eyes as the priestess resolve was set. The fact that Rowan was able to conceive a child from a water sprite might give her a better chance, but the very act of swallowing the blood of a fellow sprite would curse her. It might give her the ability of a water and a wood sprite but ultimately it would kill her slowly. Rowan clutched the small blue vile around her neck then spun around to leave. "Thank you Lum I will put this to good use I will save my son and the village, just wait and see." Lum wanted desperately to stop her, but no matter what she said, it would have made no difference. Once Rowan made her mind to do something there was no changing it. Lum could only watch in admiration as the priestess's strong back was slowly consumed by the forest. "I hope you understand what you are to give up Priestess. Once the decision is made there is no going back. I pray for your soul."

Dew clung to the grass and shined on spider webs like Christmas lights decorating the park. Sam had run all the way from her apartment in hopes to get to Isaac before Marco or any of his cronies. "Isaac!" Puffs of her warm breath floated before her, "Isaac please where are you?" Sam stood and waited, but the boy never came. She clutched the note in her pocket squeezing her fist around it. "Please tell me I'm not too late." Blindly she launched her body into the woods. "Please be there" Twigs snapped under her feet and leaves crunched as she ran deeper and deeper into the woods. The further in she ran the more everything started to look the same. Out of breath and completely lost; she caved. "Alright I give up where are you?"…"Isaac come on I know you are here somewhere" The only sounds to greet her were the wail of crickets and the occasional caw of

a crow. She took a deep breath and shouted,
"DAMN IT ISAAC... I'M LOST! ...YOU'D
BETTER COME OUT AND RESCUE ME..." Her
shoulders fell, this was pointless. She didn't know
the woods like he did and who's to say he wasn't
still safely back at the cave. "Isaac please where
are you?" She pleaded to the air. She heard a slight
rustle in a branch overhead and watched the
leaves shift as a small blue bird dove down to land
on her head. "Sederick?" She reached up pulling
the bird from its perch in her tall nest of hair and
held it level with her eyes. "Do you know where
Isaac is?" Lum nodded and took off toward the
spring.

Once again Sam allowed the small bird to
guide her through the forest. She stopped at the
sound of a chattering brook. At its edge with his
toes dug into the sandy bank sat Isaac huddled
into a ball his arms wrapped around his knees his
face buried between them. "Isaac?" He didn't
move, but she could hear him mumble something
"Umm nought Isuck"..."What?" Sam watched as
his head slowly rotated to the side to look at her
from foggy eyes, then up to the bird in the pine,
"Thanks for tattling Auntie Lum" His eyes drifted

from the bird to fall on Sam. "I'm not Isaac, I don't have a name a stupid tree was supposed to give me a name and it's dead." He shifted his face back down wiggling it further between his knees until even his ears were hidden. Sam looked up at the bird "Lum?" The bird just shrugged. Sam's eyes fell back on Isaac and she took a deep breath then sighed. She wanted to yank him from the creek by the ears if need be; she had other more pressing concerns then his little name problem. "Look who cares who was supposed to give you a name right? I know you as Isaac so you're Isaac what difference does it make who gave it to you?" She heard a muffled sniff, but nothing else; she stepped up and settled on the bank next to him and continued. "Listen you're not the only one to have it rough you know…hell I just found out I'm not even human…well technically I'm not fully human whatever that means…and I never had a home. I never had loving parents at least you have Wisteria, granted she's a grumpy old goat, but still…" She heard a stifled laugh from the boy; that brought a slight smile to her lips. "Come on" she leaned over nudging him. "I need your help, I can't do this alone." She heard another sniff and

216

watched his shoulders fall then his head lifted to stare out blankly at the flowing water. "Just my help huh? Is that all I'm good for? Doesn't anybody want me just for me?" Sam was getting a little annoyed by the boy's pity party. Lewie was in danger and she needed Isaac to get him out of it. Of course she didn't intend to hand him over to Marco; she was actually hoping he could help her rescue Lewie. But she knew it would put Isaac in danger. "Isaac listen to me I need you to come with me." He turned his head slightly looking at her with one eye "What for?" She wanted to scream why was he being so damn difficult. It wasn't like she didn't care for him. It was just that Lewie had been there for her for years, she owed him this. It should have been a no-brainer, no hesitations, risk putting Isaac in danger or letting Lewie get killed? She took a deep breath and tried to convince him to help her. If he agreed she wouldn't have to feel so guilty. "It's just something really important to me, please Isaac." The sprite prince turned his gaze away burying his face once again. "Why don't you get your boyfriend to help you." he muffled through his jeans. " Uggh...Isaac listen.." She tried reasoning with him. His hands dropped to his side his fingers dug into the soft wet sandy ground then he turned and shouted. "I said stop calling me that!" Sam pushed herself up from the ground and scowled down at him, "this is ridiculous I don't know why I thought you could help!"

"Give it up girlie" Wisteria stepped into the clearing her gaze traveled from Sam to Isaac. "What did I tell you Porty nothing but users...now girl...get lost!" Desperation took hold of Sam and she grabbed Isaac by the arm. "I'll force you if I have to!" Sam dropped Isaac's arm as the old sprite stepped closer. Without warning she kicked Isaac into the creek. "That ought to cool you off... just go with the girl at least then you'll see for yourself." Wisteria watched with cold eyes as the boy flounder in the water. Sam whipped around to yell at the old woman. "Hey what did you do that for?" Wisty turned her cold stones on Sam. "I wouldn't concern yourself with him you've got someone else who needs your help, if I've read this correctly." A wicked grin pulled at the old woman's mouth as she held up a crinkled piece of paper. "I believe you call him Lewie." Sam's eyes widened in panic when did she drop it? When did the old bat have a chance to pick it up? She tore her eyes from the crumbled note as she heard a splash in the creek and turned toward Isaac. He was standing knee deep in the stream with his arms up like a dripping scarecrow. Wisty followed her gaze to the boy then turned back to her. "Well which boy you planning on help'n huh?" She scanned the girl over with a hardened gaze then a cracked sort of laugh left her lips. "Ka ha ka ha…Can't make up your mind can you…well let me make it easy for you; there is nothing for you here and Porty doesn't need the likes of you around so why don't you go back to that boy and that woman and have yourself that family you've always dreamed of." Sam watched as Isaac drug one leg after the other from the spring and back onto the bank. As she watched her mind split; she cared for both of them, but Lewie was her brother, Isaac was just some kid she met a few weeks ago. As her mind struggled in turmoil a thought floated to the surface. Amongst the chaos Marco's voice was clear as day. *"'I can't guarantee what will happen to him…he could end up dead in a gang fight or something worse'"* Images of Lewie entered her mind, his body lay in the streets, a crimson river flowing from him. "Damn it…Isaac I'm sorry Lewie needs me now and if you won't help I'll find a way to do it myself." Isaac watched with sorrowful eyes as the girl turned away from him and ran back toward the city. Lum showed her the way.

She ran at full speed toward the club. She was so focused on getting there she hadn't noticed that Lum was no longer with her. She had run six blocks from the park then around the corner of Mary. Her body ached, but anger fueled her muscles. She kicked the back door of the club open. It was empty. "Marco where the hell are you, you bastard!?" Metal clicked across the wooden dance floor. "tsk tsk a lady shouldn't use such language Sammie, oh wait I forgot you're not really a lady are you?" A vicious grin pulled at his greasy lips. "So where's my golden goose?" Sam fought back the tears, but her eyes and face betrayed her. "Not until you tell me where you are keeping Lewie!" Marco lowered his head and shook it; then stepped over to the bar and sat down. He pulled a glass from the rack above and leaned over to pull the tap; filling his glass. He downed the contents then turned to face her.

"Now chicka that is not how this works; I can't give you what you want until you give me what I want." Sam was ready to launch at him with nothing more than her bare hands when a light tap at the door caused her to turn around. Lum was hovering by the small glass window. Sam glanced back at Marco, giving him one last dirty look before meeting with the bird outside, slamming the door behind her.

Something was stuck to the floor where Sam had stood. Marco pushed himself up from the bar and walked over picking it up. It was thin and green. He twirled it between his fingers unable to stop the grin pulling at his lips. "So you've been to the river eh my chicka?" He pinched the thin blade and it withered them crumbled between his fingers. "I guess it's time I take up fishing...ha ha ha."

A.J. Zanders

Ch. 16

Lum fluttered above Sam's head darting back and forth until the girl followed her down the street. "Wait, hold up... where are you going?" Sam was allowed to catch her breath as the bird finally stopped. She landed on a sign painted with the word Caspatcho's. "The 'Geek' brothers" she said their name as if she had just smelt something foul. "So they have Lewie?" Lum nodded then dove around the alley, Sam hot on her tail. The back door to the club was an old iron storm door. The place was once used as a bomb shelter. A large shiny new pad lock hung from a rusting metal brace. "Child's play." Sam pulled a set of tools from her pocket. Within seconds she had the door open and was immediately greeted by billows of steam that quickly filled the alley she stood in. A set of concrete steps led down into a narrow passage. The walls were lined with black pipes like the veins of some monster. They swelled and pulsed as they pushed steam from the joints when the pressure became too great. With each release she could hear an agonizing scream…. "Lewie!"

Sam followed the pipes down the passage. The further she went the darker it became and the louder the moans until she came to a door. A sliver of red light floated eerily on the steam at her feet. Again there was a pad lock she worked the tumblers quickly and shoved the heavy door with all her might it swung open only to fall from its hinges. "Ah!" .A heavy breath escaped her lips. "That was close." She turned her attention from the door to the black veins overhead; they grew thicker and they seemed to be coming from everywhere. They merge at the center of the room where a massive black metal heart stood pumping large quantities of scolding hot water throughout the building. ..."Aaaaahhhhhhhh!" Sam's light brown eyes shot toward the center of the room. "CAT!" The pipes rumbled and the massive metal body belched out a cloud of steam, ripping another scream from Lewie's throat. He had been stripped down to his boxers and strapped to the metal beast from behind. Tears threatened to fall as Sam witnesses the torment of her brother. "Marco you bastard how could you...you two were friends?" She approached him slowly; however fear held her at the ankles she did not want to see what his body looked like after so much torture. "Lewie....Cat?" ...As the steam rose to the ceiling she could see that he was covered in dark red almost purple skin; it had turned brown where his flesh touch the scorching metal. His eyes were white the color had rolled to the back of his head. He didn't respond to her calls; his breath was erratic and his screams seemed only to be a reflex.

Sam stepped a little closer reaching her hand out slowly to Lewie's face, but stopped inches from contact. His long beautiful hair stuck to his forehead and cheeks in jagged chunks. The rest lay scattered around his feet. She drew her hand back clenching it near her chest. She swallowed hard at the giant lump in her throat. She fought back the tears as she thought about the smug little Sicilian hacking away at Lewie's dark locks. "Marco you bastard!"

Once again her fingers hovered by his sweating face as she gathered the courage to touch him. His cheeks were blistered and swollen. The ball in her throat grew bigger every second, as her finger uncurled. "Don't touch him!" Sam froze then spun around to find Isaac standing in the doorway. "What are you doing here I thought you didn't wanted to help me." Isaac waved the girl's question away and stepped up near the body hanging against the boiler. He climbed up on a broken crate and stared him right in the face. The man only stared blankly through half lidded eyes. After a minute or two Isaac took a deep breath then reached inside his pocket pulling out a small jar filled with some thick yellow substance. "Here!" he said holding it out to her. Sam scrutinized his face. She had seen this look before.

In an instant he would switch from a sniffling child to a hardened old man; one who had lived through Nam and had somehow kept his sanity. At that moment she stared caramel to aqua at the old man. She shook off his cool gaze. "Why are you here?" she pressed, uncertain if he knew what he had gotten himself in to. "He came with me." Sam lifted her eyes slowly to the familiar voice. Leaning against the door frame, was the short Sicilian, with greased black hair. "Marco?" Sam was speechless, why was Isaac with him? "It looks like your little hero here asked to stand in your friend's place. I must thank you Sam by luring him here it saved me the trouble of looking for the little golden goose." Marco stepped through the threshold and rested a hand on Isaac's shoulder then leaned done to whisper in his ear. "She's a cute one isn't she…too bad she was just using you to get her lover back" For a moment Sam saw the flash of the sniffling child in Isaac's eyes then it vanished shoved to the back of his subconscious and locked away. "Isaac?" The boy turned away from her and headed out stepping over the steel door. "Don't listen to anything he says Isaac…it's not like that." She protested. Isaac stopped turning around just long enough to toss the jar to her. "That will take away his pain...Goodbye Sam" His eyes shifted from anger to sorrow then back to anger and finally settled somewhere between on hurt. Sam looked from his pain-filled eyes to the jar in her hand. When she lifted her eyes back up, the boy had run down the dark corridor and disappeared. "ISAAC!"

"That's pointless Sammie a boy's heart is just so fragile" he made sort of a mock pity sound with his lips then looked from the door frame to the body still hanging from the boiler. "I suggest you take your baggage and get out of my sight, I have what I want now. So long as you are a good girl and keep the cops out of this I promise not to rough him up too much." His stubbled lip curled back flashing a gold tooth. "It was a pleasure." He turned to leave her with Lewie's burnt and blistered body. "Marco, you bastard, come back here!" Marco paused momentarily spinning around to give her a malicious grin. "You don't know how right you are." He turned and walked away shedding any need for her with each click of his heels.

"Nnnh" A faint moan drew her attention from the door to the man still hanging against the boiler. "Damn it!" She stared at the jar a few more seconds before setting it down. Watching the steam rise around Lewie's body, she knew she would have to do something fast. Her gaze fell on a valve against the opposite wall. "Hold on Lewie I'm getting you out of here!" Sam stepped over to the valve; a cloud of steam hovered ominously over the lever as if it was daring her to try. A quick scan of the room told her there was nothing she could use to protect her hands. Taking a deep breath, she peeled off her shirt and wrapped it around her hands. If Lewie had been conscious he would have seen the long scars slashed along her back and shoulders. For just a moment she was thankful he was unconscious. Despite her best effort the wheel would not turn. The rumble of water grew louder as it made its way back toward the boiler. Her thin t-shirt was not much protection against the scorching metal; the heat soaked through burning her hands. "Come on damn it turn!"

The water rushed to the massive black heart, steam rose all around, but it did not elicit another scream from Lewie. The room filled with a cloud of white mist that sent goose bumps rushing across her bare skin. "It's cold?"… "Samantha…can you hear me…Samantha?" Sam scanned the room for another person, but there was no one. "Who…?" A soft chuckle rang throughout the pipes. "My you are forgetful." Sam's face lit up as she recognized the voice…"Ren!. Ren is that you?"…"Yes and I can only keep the temperature down for a few more minutes. You have to untie him and quickly!" Sam looked about the pipes still wondering from where his majesty's voice was coming. Another moan from Lewie pulled her back to the boiler. "I'll get you down Cat just hang on!" Pulling the tools from her pocket, she began sawing away at the zip ties binding Lewie's hands. The plastic had melted into his wrist and his hands were swollen. Tears spilt forth over her lashes as she tried to free his bonds. "You're an idiot, why didn't you just leave here" The plastic snapped as the metal tools made their way through. A muffled thump followed as Lewie's body slid to the ground.

"Samantha quickly, cover as much of his body with that salve as you can and get him out of here.

As soon as I leave these pipes the water temperature is going to rise again"

Sam looked down at Lewie's six feet one inch, one hundred and eighty pound frame and wanted to cry."How? There is no way I could carry him... look at me." There was a brief pause then the boiler rumbled again. "Hmm...Samantha, do you think you could move his body a few feet away from the boiler?" Sam looked from the boiler down to Lewie's body. "Yeah I think so, but what good would that do?" ... "I have an idea it could work so long as our friend here stay's unconscious." The boiler rumbled again belching out a blob of water. Once it hit the wet concrete it slithered toward Lewie's body. Out of reflex Sam reached to pull Lewie away...A familiar face formed within the water, "It is alright child I can help him." Sam glance at the features formed out of water, it smiled awkwardly. She nodded then backed away from her brother's body. A pool quickly gathered around Lewie and began to recede underneath him until the floor was completely dry. "Ngh...ou..." Slowly Lewie's lashes fluttered open revealing bright blue eyes. Sam rushed to his side, "Lewie...you're ok!"

Lewie blinked at her with curious blue orbs. "Wow am I that difficult *cough* to remember."…"Ren…you possessed Lewie's body…how cool!...wait you're going to give it back to him right?"

A faint smile pulled at Lewie's mouth, but she could tell that was the sprite's grin on Lewie's face. "Yes Samantha, to both your questions, but please, the salve. He is in immense pain." he whispered through nearly still lips. His lids closed again and his breathing became slow and soft. Panic raced through Sam's mind. "Ren!"…"I'm fine just please hurry"

Sam quickly pried the wax seal from the jar. A rancid smell of rotting flesh and vomit assaulted her nose causing her stomach to lurch forward. She held the jar at arm's length trying not to breathe it in. "What is this crap?...ugh it smells awful!" She heard a faint chuckle, "It's one of Wisty's specialties *cough* maybe you should ask her *cough* although I don't think you really want to know."

Sam pulled her shirt from around her hands and quickly wrapped it around her face. Empting the contents of the jar onto Lewie's body, she smeared it along his chest and down his limbs. It was warm and slimy, just knowing how it smelt as she pushed it around caused her stomach to flip again. "Ugh this stuff feels as gross as it smells!" She felt every muscle in Lewie's body twitch his face twisting as her fingers glided along his skin. She felt the heat rise in her cheeks and she shook it away. "Ngh" …"Ren…is it working are you ok?" Lewie's left arm shot up to hover over his face. He turned it over back to front staring at it. Barely visible was a white ring of skin around his forth finger. *Mmm* …. "Ren are you listening can you stand?" The sprite king peeled the pale swollen fingers from his vision and locked eyes with the girl. "Yes we should leave. We need to take his body to the springs; it is the only way he will recover from this much damage." Sam hesitated, "But what about Isaac…we can't just leave him!"

Ren lifted Lewie's six feet one inch stature to his fullest height and immediately regretted it. He felt the rush of blood and saw the black walls of dizziness close around him. "Why do humans have to be so tall?" he grumbled, his hand flew up to his forehead and the other shot out to steady himself on a pillar. "Ren!" Sam reached over to

233

steady him. Ren shuffled around to face the girl; struggling to remain standing on his unfamiliar feet. He rested his hands on her shoulders as much for connection as balance. Staring down into her caramel eyes, he mused, *she really does take after her mother.* Shaking the thought from his mind he tried to focus on the matter at hand. "Samantha if we don't get your friend to the springs immediately he will die..." his gaze drifted away to a pile of soaked fire wood on the floor, " ...besides Isaac can take care of himself they won't hurt him so long as they can use him" He said the last bit more to comfort himself than Sam. The girl's face drew into a scowl, "But he's your son don't you care!" Ren pulled his fixed gaze from the pile and focused on Sam his normal soft playful look had hardened, "Come we need to leave" ...Sam was hesitant. "But..." Ren shook her shoulders lightly forcing her to think of their current situation. "Your friend does mean something to you doesn't he?" Sam felt the tension in her chest and she breathed deep. "Yeah, he's my brother." Lewie's face pulled back into a wrinkled smile that shown in Ren's bright blue eyes. "Then we really should hurry!" Sam nodded,

"but we come back for Isaac once Lewie is safe."…
"Of course"

A.J. Zanders

Ch. 17

"Fire will consume our world "

The light pestered her tired eyes as she knelt in the dirt at the base of a burnt fossil of a tree. Her nails were black and chipped the hole at her feet was barely a foot deep. "Damn, where did that woman bury it?" She let her head fall back to stare up at the light dancing through the tree tops. "Ugh"

A bright orange leaf snapped free and floated down to rest on her forehead. "It's getting close…how many autumns has it been now?" She turned her head toward the bluebird as it landed on a branch just behind her. "So where is the boy?" The small bird looked away; Isaac had asked her not to tell Wisteria where he had gone, but she couldn't help but worry about him. Lum's feathers fluffed as the boys words came back to her again.

Isaac stood outside the edge of the forest something clutched in his hand. "Thank you for telling me where she went Lum." His eyes traveled toward the city a look of resolve settled on his features. He squeezed the vile in his pocket and nodded to Lum, "I'm going to fix all this I don't want to be used anymore…I'll make sure I am no use to anyone." Lum blinked her copper eyes and tipped her tiny head slightly what on earth was he planning. Isaac pressed a finger to his lips, "Don't tell Wisty ok…I know she would try to stop me, you understand don't you?" Lum watched as the boy walked away. She never longed for her old body more than right now. She wished she had the arms to reach out and hold him; to keep him from going, to erase his pain, but she could only watch. The visions she saw so many years ago flashed before her mind's eye. The

*unstoppable flames causing anguish and pain to echo
from the boy's lips as they slowly consumed him. No!
She shook the image from her head, cursing her gift.
Why had that been the future she for saw for the boy.
She took a deep breath and followed him. Maybe he
found a way to avoid such a horrible fate.*

Lum turned her beady eyes on the small hole
at the base of the burnt tree then back toward
Wisteria; the old woman looked as if she had been
up all night. Lum reluctantly shook her head, to
the woman's previous question. "Ka ha ha, you
don't have to tell me; he went after that girl didn't
he?… Foolish boy. Don't worry I'm aware of it.
Who do you suppose gave him the salve for that
man…It was good you came back to tell me what
happened." Lum looked away avoiding the old
woman's piercing eye, she felt like a spy. In certain
ways it was useful to be a bird and Lum had
gotten used to it, but just in the past few weeks
she missed having the strength to do more.

Something moved amongst the leaves and the
two shifted their gaze toward the sound. It grew
louder and was soon accompanied by moans of
pain. Sam was practically pulling Lewie's body
through the leaves like a plow. "I'm sorry Lewie,

Ren I can't do this anymore." Sam dropped from exhaustion Lewie slipped from her grasp and she collapsed to the ground next to him.

"What did I tell you girl? Didn't I tell you not to come back here and why have you brought another human with you?"
Lewie's head lifted slowly as he gingerly pushed himself off the ground. Wisteria took one look at his brilliant blue eyes shining past strands of choppy brown hair and laughed. "Ka ha ha you old fool possessed a human body did you and a mess of a one by the look of ya...Ka ha ha." Ren released a soft embarrassed chuckle. Wisteria stepped over to the spent water sprite and sneered at him. "Gone and worn yourself out, have yeah? Well don't expect my help." Wisteria turned on her heels to head deeper into the forest.
Sam knelt in the debris clutching leaves in her fist. How could the old bat just walk away and leave him like this? "Hey wait a second you can't just leave me like this I don't think I can carry him much further!" The old woman's hand went into the air and waved. "Not my problem girlie."
"Ooo you old bat!" Sam wanted to use the last of her strength to throw something at the old bitty,

but was stopped by Ren's voice. "Samantha, leave her...we need to get Lewie's...ngh"..."Ren...Ren!" Lewie's body slipped into unconsciousness. "Lewie!"...Sam tried to wake him but as she nudged his shoulder his skin curled and peeled under her touch. "Oh god! Cat hang on!" Lum quickly landed on the man's head and began pecking at it, hopping up and down with her tiny feet.

"What are you doing you crazy bird!...Stop that!" Sam tried to shoo her away, but her wrist was caught by one of Lewie's massive hands. "Sam it's ok"

That voice? ..."Cat?"

A faint smile pulled at the corner of his mouth, that wasn't Ren's impish grin, no it was Lewie's own sweet smile. "Cat! But how?"

"Ren told me he can't run my body while also trying to heal it, I think I have enough strength to get us to the falls...if you wouldn't mind giving me your shoulder for a while longer...I'm sorry for the condition I'm in...unh... you must be pretty grossed out."

Sam just shook her head and slid her arm under his. "You must be crazy if you think I've carried you this far and I'm going to give up on you now" "Thank you Sam."

Four long shadows moved along the wall as the iridescent bulb swung overhead. "It was so nice of you to come all this way little man...It saved us the trouble of going into that forest to look for yous." Johnny squatted down eye level with the empty sea that was Isaac's eyes.
"That old woman you've been hanging around has been given us all sorts of trouble" He pointed one of his sausage fingers at a man drooling on himself in the corner. "He ain't been the same since that witch got a hold of him" Isaac's lifeless eyes slid over to the man; he was thin and hunched and his eyes seemed to chase invisible butterflies. "See completely loony" Johnny

retorted. Isaac turned back to stare into the round shiny face of the Grecian without so much as a change in his expression.

 "Hey Jimmy are you sure he's like that girlie our great-grandfather had at his shop?"
Jimmy waltzed over grabbing a handful of Isaac's hair and yanked his head back blowing a thick cloud of cigar smoke from between his teeth into the boy's face. "Yeah I'm certain...look at him does he look human to you?" He pushed Isaac's head back down and looked at Johnny.
"Well?"..."No but, he ain't done nothing yet he's been sitting in this pool of dirt all tied up and nothing is growing."

  "Hey hands off the merchandise I don't want you damaging my golden goose now!" Marco stepped past the Greek brothers brushing Jimmy's hand aside.
"Marco? You said this kid here could grow us more product then that sassy little tart you were keeping"
Isaac flinched slightly. In response to Isaac's reaction Johnny decide to rub salt in a little deeper and began making baby faces at him. "Ah what's the matter? The mere mention of that wench pulls

on your heart strings? Well why don't we bring her back here? Wouldn't that cheer you up, oh wait that's right she has someone else she's more concerned about doesn't she?" …Isaac empty eyes flashed into icy emeralds. For a split second the Grecian was nervous. "Hey Marco this kids creeping me out make him do something already." Isaac slid his murky aqua pools toward Marco. "So what's it gonna be kid? Are you going to cooperate or do I need to tap you like a maple?" Marco pulled a switch blade from his pocket Lifeless puddles stared at him then Isaac slowly looked away…"Have it your way."

A sharp pain sunk into his ankles as Marco drove the knife in further. "We don't need your cooperation my friend… your blood will do the work for us." A warm liquid trickled down Isaac's ankles then ran down the slope of his foot. He felt it run between his toes and into the ground beneath his feet. Greenish yellow cotyledons sprouted up so quickly that two palmate leaves burst forth followed by two more. In the matter of minutes Isaac sat in the middle of a full lush green garden. Johnny stared in amazement at the pool of dirt now overflowing with deep green plants then walked over smacking Marco on the back. "Holy Shit! Marco you weren't kidding it would take us three years to get these plants this full and all it took this kid was a few drops of blood."

Although impressed Jimmy wasn't as quick to celebrate, "So what is your angle Marco why give us this kid for a mere portion of our turf?" Marco's hand flew up to his chest and tried to look pained, "I'm hurt Jimmy, you don't trust me? He is merely a peace offering between our two territories." Jimmy gave Marco a suspicious look, "It feels more like a Trojan horse to me." Marco waved Jimmy's concerns away, "Please don't get me wrong he's as much mine as he is yours I'm just letting you have him first. It's the least I could do for getting rid of that worthless Valentino for me."

Marco's conditioned eyes noticed something move outside the window. One didn't spend their life hiding from authority without recognizing a sign of danger approaching. He gave it an inconspicuous glance. *Huh earlier than I expected.* "Well boys enjoy your little meal ticket while it is your turn I shall return for him later" Marco gave a dramatic bow before escaping out the front door. He had made it out just in time. A minute later, clouds of purple smoke bellowed from the windows as the Greek brothers made a desperate attempt to air out the room. A vicious grin spread across Marco's face as he walked away to wait for the old woman to finish the dirty work for him.

Ch. 18

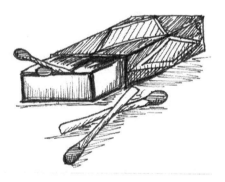

The room quickly filled with smoke the basement's narrow windows provided poor ventilation. The virulent fumes invaded the Greek brother's lungs and burned their skin. Their eyes and throat felt raw as road rash. It was as if they were coughing fire from their lungs. Their stomachs cramped doubling them over in fits of vomit before they finally curled up on the floor like dead ants. Isaac watched as the two men convulsed violently then dropped to the ground; their fingers still twitching.

"Well now they lasted longer than I thought; tough little cockroaches" Isaac shifted his gaze to an old woman standing at the threshold. Her eyes drifted from the two men on the floor to the boy tied in the center of a green pool. ..."And I see your immunity is as strong as ever...good...*cough*...Hmmm guess I'm a bit more sensitive then I remember." Wisteria placed a cloth over her mouth and stepped into the room. Blinking at the old sprite, Isaac watched as her frizzy gray hair blurred then faded His eyes closed and he slumped over in the chair.
"Ka ha ha guess not even you could take this high a dose ....Oh well"

Sam looked down at Lewie's sleeping form in amazement even the scars were gone. "Wow you are amazing Ren!" Being in his full water form Sam couldn't tell that the swirl of water in his face was the equivalent of a human blush. "Well, it doesn't come without a price, I'll be out of commission for a while I don't think I could even possess a fish right now." …Sam laughed it felt so good at the moment that she had almost forgotten about one other person. "Wait Ren, we still have to save Isaac. I can't do it by myself" Ren's bright blue eyes cast down to his own reflection in the pool; bright blue spheres blinked back at him from a distorted figure. "I'm sorry Samantha I don't think I am going to be much use to anyone for a while."

Sam looked down at Lewie's body and the feeling of hopelessness welled back up into her chest. She only escaped from the Greek brother's club because Ren was there to help her; not to mention Marco was practically handing him over. How could she possibly pry Isaac from the Sicilian's grubby fingers. Rescuing Lewie was one thing, but Marco was not going to give Isaac up so easily.

"What am I supposed to do?!"

"You have gotten too heavy for me to carry boy." Wisteria set Isaac's body down to rest for a bit. She was halfway across the city; the park was only a few blocks away. "Well, we aren't going to get there by standing around now are we?" She took a couple of deep breaths then squatted down to haul the boy onto her back once again. A voice from behind stopped her mid pickup and she spun around to face it. "And just where do you think you are taking my little golden goose? Although maybe I should be thanking you, dealing with the Greek brothers for me and all; however, I can't just let you walk away with my prized possession now can I?"

Wisteria slowly lowered Isaac back down to reach inside her pocket. "If you want him so bad why don't you come and get him?" Marco smirked he was fully aware of what the old sprite had in store. "Hag just how stupid do you think I am? Ever since I was old enough to sit up on my own my grandfather told me stories of your kind. I didn't keep Sam around for her looks you know... although I must thank you for giving away your only daughter. She's been very useful, but I'd be a fool to settle for a lowly half sprite like her, when I can have the prince of all sprites." Marco pulled a pistol from his jacket and pointed it at Wisteria's head. Her hand relaxing inside her pocket as shock spread across her face. How did he know about her, about her daughter, surly it wasn't just from some old man's stories?

"How did you know all that?...Who are you anyway?" Wisteria never took her eyes off the human. "What's the matter couldn't you tell?" his smirk widening. "Sammie and I aren't so different except I didn't receive her wonderful gift." His smile faded and he pulled back the hammer. "Now hand over my golden goose and I will let you go back to your daughter in one piece."

Wisteria looked down at the boy still unconscious from the drug then back to the man pointing a gun at her. "Fine, but let me at least kick him once more." The man's eyebrow went up and an evil laugh ripped from his lips. "You really are a stone cold old hag aren't you?" Wisteria turned around giving Isaac a quick nudge with her foot. To Marco it looked as if the old woman just couldn't muster up any more power than that. Wisteria turned back briefly a withered grin on her face then she stepped over Isaac's body and hobbled away as if the kick had injured her tired feet.

"Ha ha ha, that all you got old woman?" Marco mocked her as he let the wave of victory wash over him.

When he could no longer see her she bent down to pick up a small vial she had kicked from Isaac's body and had been shoving it along the ground with her "injured" foot until now. "Your mother never intended this for you, child…it wouldn't have worked the way you wanted it to anyway. I'm afraid you misread your mother's memories." She held the small blue vial up and sighed. It was a one-time shot and it would cost her. She closed her fist around it and shoved it in her pocket. "You are on your own now Porty. I never really wanted you to face that fate either, just so you know." She tossed her head back to look up at the stars. "I suppose I'm a coward after all."

Lum led the way out of the forest; the park light shined out in greeting and Sam set foot on the soft wet grass of the park. A huddled figure shuffled along toward them until it was illuminated completely by the lamppost. "Wisteria!...did you go after Isaac...where is he?" The old sprite avoided the girl's eyes and tried to step around her. Sam cut her off. "Damn it old woman are you going to answer me?!" Wisteria said nothing and stepped around her.

"Answer me!" Sam reached out grabbing Wisteria by the shoulder. "Hey! I'm talking to you!" Wisteria spun around; the light glistened off tiny droplets at the corners of her eyes. Brushing Sam's hand away, she grumbled a response "He's on his own now...leave him." Sam retaliated by running in front of the old sprite blocking her escape. "Wait a minute you cold hearted old bitch!"…*SLAP* Once again Sam felt the sting of calloused skin across her cheek, but somehow it felt welcomed. It was different then all those times Marco had struck her.

"That is no way to speak to your mother!" Wisteria withdrew her hand surprised at herself. No matter how insolent the boy had been she never once slapped him, but this girl…Sam stood dumbfounded, holding her stinking cheek. "Mother?" Wisteria locked eyes with her for a moment. The message was clear, *move or this will not be a pleasant reunion.* Sam stepped aside unable to force the words up through her throat. Wisteria did not look back as she walked through the open path and away from Sam. She paused still facing the darkness, "I'm sorry Samantha…I'm sorry for everything you have ever gone through. Please take care of Isaac for me." Tears threatened at the edge of her lids, "Wait you old goat!...Wisteria!... Mom! Please wait. Why did you abandon me? I have a right to know?!" she screamed after the old woman. Lum dove between them, before Sam could take another step toward her mother. "Get

out of the way Lum I have a right to know."
Lumeria looked from the girl to the old woman
and her heart sank. She shook the fate of the old
sprite from her mind and quickly flew up to pull
on Sam's sleeve urging her into the city. Sam
peeled her eyes away from the hunch form fading
in the distance to the small bird. "Right, I'm sorry
Lum we need to save Isaac"

"I see you are finally awake good you can stand
on your own" Marco set Isaac down on the step to
fish for his keys. As Isaac stood outside the two
heavy black doors of Club Enchant he placed his
hand inside his front pocket. He only had one
thing left in his collection and it wasn't what he
thought it would be. Instead of a small glass vial it
felt like an acorn. He clutched it in his fist before
pulling it out and dropping it on the step. Marco
quickly turned on the sound "What was that?"

Isaac stared blankly at the anxious Sicilian. Marco squinted suspiciously at the boy then turned his distrusting eyes down the streets, before roughly grabbing the small sprite by the arm and shoving him inside.

The room was barren nothing but concrete with a steel chair in the middle. Marco tossed Isaac into the back furthest from the door and smiled. "You are all mine now…with the Greek brother's out of the way and Mr. B taking the rap for Lewie's kidnapping there is no one to stand in my way. I can rake in all the dough for myself…I don't even have to share it with that back stabbing partner of mine." He looked the boy over rubbing his knuckles. Isaac thought he looked as if he was ready to eat him and maybe he wasn't too far off. "I wonder what the prince of sprites taste like, I'm sure a little wouldn't hurt." Marco roughly pulled up Isaac's sleeve then wrapped his finger around his smooth arm. Something tingled then burned his arm where Marco's grip tightened. A wicked grin pulled at Marco's lips. "Oh yes very nice…the water from your blood is delicious indeed, better than any plant's or human's I've ever tasted." He then pulled Isaac up from the floor and secured him to the chair. "Get comfortable my little money maker, you'll be here awhile."

Marco turned away to peer out the door; the club was quite. Mr. B was currently at the police station and with him gone the girls were out doing their own thing. The club was completely empty. For now the club was his domain. He smiled to himself as he shut the door on his prize.

Lights reflected off the row of shining windows. A cloud of smoke filled the streets. Sam turned the corner to find three fire trucks, an ambulance and four police cars blocking her way. She shoved through the crowd to the yellow tape tied between two lampposts. Lum watched the smoke crawl along the blacken brick and visions older than the city played before her. *Is this what I saw?* Her tiny head jerked down to the sound of the girl screaming the boy's name. "ISAAC!".... Sam froze as she watched the smoke drift from the broken windows of Caspatcho. Two gurneys were pushed from the building by men in blue jump suits. "ISAAC!" Sam pushed past the remaining police shaking off their attempts to stop her. "Wait please! Is there…" she swallowed hard, "…was there a little boy in there?" The man in the blue jumpsuit pulled a black glove from one of his hands and patted her lightly on the head. "I'm sorry sweetheart we are still evacuating we have only found these two so far so for now please miss why don't you go home." Another man in a yellow fire suit shouted to the rest, "We have another one…looks to me like a child!"

Sam wanted to scream. Bolting for the remains of the building, she came to an abrupt halt as two strong arms wrapped around her and pulled her away from the burnt and blackened remains. "Stop let me go my friend could be in there … LET ME GO DAMN IT!" She kicked and screamed against her retainer, but to no avail.

"Miss relax please we are doing everything we can."

The police officer's grip slacked and Sam broke free turning on him. ..."He's just a kid Damn it...I never should have..."

"Miss?" he reached out to comfort her, but Sam smacked his hand away then ran from the noise and chaos. A block away her legs gave under her and she crumbled. "He can't...*hick* he can't...it's all my fault..."

Lum flew from a roof top to land in front of the weeping girl. There wasn't much a small bird could do to comfort a human, especially when she was just as upset. She hopped over nudging the girl's knee with her soft feathered head. *Please don't cry...I believe he is still alive he must be* Sam peered past tear stained hands smeared with mascara to stare down at the small blue bird. "You can talk?" Lum nodded, *I can speak to any sprite, human or animal if I choice.* Lum watched the girl's features twist in confusion. *It's a long story...and it doesn't matter right now... look.* The small bird dropped a piece of yarn near the girl's foot, *see I know he is ok...somehow I don't think he was caught in the fire.* Sam picked the piece of yarn from the ground and looked hurt and angry. "How is this supposed to be proof he is alive, and how come you never spoke to me before and what was with all the head pecking? That really hurt you know" Lum didn't answer she merely hopped up and glided down to the next corner. When Sam caught up to her; Lum was holding a bright pink bendy straw in her beak. "Great you have found some good nesting materials how is that helping?!" Lum shook her head and dropped the straw then flew to the next corner; there she picked up a *Sobe* bottle cap that said *It's all about the lizard* "Very nice, but this isn't time to start a collection either." Once again Lum dropped the cap and flew down the street. "Gods you are one crazy bird." Sam followed. This time Lum landed near an earring that looked incredible familiar. "Hey that's my earring is this where I lost it?" She reached up touching her naked ear.

Don't you see? These are Isaac's most treasured things. He's been leaving us a trail. Sam picked up the earring to examine it. "So he took my earring." Lum flew up pecking the girl directly in the forehead. "Hey!" *...We have to hurry!*

Running to the end of Isaac's trail they stopped in front of an all too familiar place. *Club Enchant* flickered in purple neon above two black ominous doors. Sam felt something crunch under her foot as she made her way down the steps. "What the…" Lifting her foot, she revealed a partially crushed acorn. She peeled pieces from the sole of her shoe and picked the rest off the concrete step. It still had enough shell to wobble slightly in her hand. Lum landed in the girl's hand and examined the acorn. *He's here.* Sam looked at the small bird then back to the double doors. "Ok then let's get him out of there."

Sam pulled and she shoved but the doors were locked tight. "Why is the club closed?" She wanted to bang on the doors, scream for Marco to get his ass out here and give Isaac back, but what good would that do really? Her tantrum was stopped by a light tug at her collar. Lum flew off around the building and Sam followed. There was a single door with a simple lock at the back of the club. "Piece of cake."

Reaching into her pocket, she expected to find long metal tools; but her eyes widened as her fingers groped nothing but squares of cotton. Despair consumed her; the tools were back at the Greeks' club, currently burnt to ash. "DAMN IT!"

She banged her fist in frustration against the steel door. The pieces of the acorn rattled in her palm. She leaned back and opened her hand staring at the pieces. She wanted to plead with it to help her but what could an acorn do. She closed her fingers around it and wiped her eyes; tears slipped between her fingers.

"I wish you could help me." She secretly pleaded with the tiny seed. A second later she felt something move beneath her fingers. "What the?" She opened her hand to reveal the acorn had sprouted. "But how...I can't..."

Lum fluttered excitedly around her. *Quick get the acorn to sprout further and have it unlock the door.* Sam looked from the small seedling to the bird, "What but I don't even know how I did this?" *Just try.* Sam placed the budding sprout on the ground under the door and held her hand over it pleading with it to grow. "Please grow, Isaac needs our help"

The seedling wiggled up between her fingers then darted under the door. Lum and Sam waited uncertain if the new sapling would be capable of turning a lock or if Sam were even capable of getting it to understand her. Within seconds they heard a *click* and the door inched open. Sam's heart raced with excitement she had done it. *It must have been that plant I kept in my room the one my mother left with me now that I don't have it*...Sam thought. The door swung open to a hairy chest in a black silk button up shirt and tan leather jacket. "Sammie my chicka… I thought I told you to be a good girl."

A.J. Zanders

Ch. 19

"Our people will be free"

Her spotted leathery hand rested shakily on the old elm tree. "I'm sorry sister I tried, but the boy is just so stubborn…I should have done this a long time ago." Wisteria pulled the cork from the blue vial and opened her mouth to toss down the eerie liquid inside, but centuries and turned the contents into dry powder, when nothing had trickled out Wisteria peer in with one amber eye. "What!" She wanted to crush the bottle in anger and desperation. A small gourd at her hip sloshed as she moved. "Well I suppose two hundred years buried under a tree would dry it up." She pulled the stopper on the gourd and poured its burgundy liquid carefully into the small vial then replaced its cork and shook it.

"Ah there we go" Pulling the stopper, she downed the tiny swallow of red glowing liquid. "Ah never thought a water sprite would taste so good...ugh!" Her stomach cramped and twisted; her blood felt like it was on fire. It took a moment for the pain to subside; when she could stand up straight again she tussled her pink and violet hair and took a deep breath; everything was in focus. "It sure feels good to be young again even if it is only for a few minutes. ...Well better get to work." She pulled a knife from her pouch and slit her wrist across then down to each palm letting the blood pool. Pressing her bleeding hands into the trunk of the elm, she felt her body go numb. "I couldn't do anything for you back then Autumn so I hope this makes up for it." Her blood raced through the maze of bark, then disappeared at the center. It was so difficult to keep her eyes open; her body grew heavy and started to slip down the tree trunk. "If you meet that little brat give him a swift kick from me...ok." Her head came to rest on the roots of the elm. The hard rough bark began to soften and she found herself resting on a warm lap. Wisteria looked up into dark red irises. "I'm so glad to see you again Autumn." A tired hand reached up to touch the woman's face. "Look at you, you're so old." She cackled. Autumn smiled softly, "look who's talking." Wisteria's hand slipped from her sister's face and her lids closed slowly, a weak smile pulled at her lips. "I'm grateful that the last thing I get to see is your smile...Take care Autumn, I'm sorry I couldn't get to you sooner." Wisteria's smile faded and her head rolled slowly to the side her breathing stopped. "Oh Wisty."

"Let go you bastard!"

Sam struggled against Marco's grip but the more
she struggled the harder he squeezed the tiny bird
in his other hand. Painful shrills were forces from
Lum's beak as she was clutched between his
fingers. ...."Just let the bird go it has nothing to do
with me." An evil knowing grin pulled at Marco's
features. "Tsk tsk...seriously Sammie you must
take me for a fool...I've seen this little bird
hanging around you and that little golden goose. I
can't let him go and tell someone else where you
are now can I?"

Sam's heart fell; she wanted to make it up to
Isaac by saving him from this but instead she got
herself caught as well. The heavy pull of
hopelessness drained her strength. She struggled
to reignite her hatred. "You're working on a
record Marco three kidnappings in one day."

"Three? But my chicka you are the first...that
little golden goose walked right into my arms."
Sam glared at him. "Oh you must mean Lewie..."
He tried to look pained, "... that wasn't me...you
can thank the Greek brothers or rather I should
thank them. I didn't have to lift a finger and
thanks to that old hag I didn't have to do a thing.
All my problems were neatly taken care of...that is

of course except for you." His crooked smile grew wider. Sam always knew Marco was twisted and a bit evil, but now he just looked completely mad. She couldn't hide the uncontrollable fear that wrapped its way around her spine manipulating her features. Marco laughed. "What's the matter my chicka you should be happy. I've decided to keep you both." He looked from Sam to the bird in his hand. "However this I don't need." He squeezed the tiny bird so hard Sam heard a slight pop then the bird went still. "LUM!"…"You bastard! I swear I'm going to kill you, she didn't do anything to you."

"I'd like to see you try my chicka" Marco pushed open the door shoving Sam inside. Isaac was tied to a steel chair. Tubes protruded from his body like a spider's legs. Each pulsating limb sent more and more of his blood into small plastic bags. "Ha… ha…see I told you I wouldn't kill him." Sam turned on Marco wishing to god looks really could kill, because at that moment Marco would have drop dead with that twisted smirk still frozen on his face… "Careful now Sammie you might hurt my feelings…ha … ha… ha."

The door slammed behind him. She could hear his sick laughter fade as he turned the corner. Sam peeled her glare from the door and rushed over to Isaac. She began pulling the tubes from his arms; he didn't even look up at her. He just stared at his bare feet with empty eyes. "Isaac, come on Isaac say something!" She shook him by the shoulders repeating his name. He continued to stare blank and lifeless. "Damn it Isaac….you're a real idiot you know that?"

He flinched and his eyes widened to a click of the door knob. Sam turned around as the door crept open. Marco stood at the door long enough to toss the small bird onto the stone floor. "I almost forgot…you can have this back now"

"Lum!" Sam released Isaac and dove for the bird. She bent down cupping the bird's tiny body between her hands. She held her to her chest and cried. "I'm so sorry Lum"…

"You are the child of a human and a sprite, are you not?" Sam shifted slightly toward an unfamiliar voice coming from the boy tied to the chair. "Isaac?" Isaac smiled a remorseful sad smile. "I always was fond of that name, I'm so glad he likes it." Sam stared bewildered at the boy as a voice most unfitting left his lips. "Who... who are you?" Isaac laughed in a deep feminine tone, "I am the boy's mother..." Isaac's head tilted slightly at the girl's quizzical look, "... it is a long story child." Dark green eyes peered down into the girl's hands and soft blue lips pulled into a frown. "Oh Lum you never did learn did you child. That's how you ended up that way in the first place." Sam felt anger rise past the despair, heat burned in her chest. "Hey what is with you she's dying maybe already dead and all you can do is ridicule her." The boy's expression hardened, "Serves her right. She never did know when to butt out."

Sam stood up and slapped the boy then jerked her hand back as if she had just placed it on a hot stove. "I'm sorry Isaac... Wait, no, no I'm not this is all, your fault. We wouldn't be in this mess in the first place if you hadn't been an idiot!" She wanted to slap him again but was stopped by the harsh female voice. "Listen to me, am I right in believing you are the child from a union between a sprite and a human?" Sam turned away avoiding his eyes. It was disturbing enough that the voice was not his own, and now someone else stared at her through his eyes. He had given her that look twice before and it sent chills down her spine; now she knew from where it had come. "That's what I was told, so what?"

"Good." The boy wiggled an arm free and pulled it around to rest in his lap palm up. He opened his hand revealing an old pocket knife. " I took this from that foolish human. Now listen to me take this and slit that bird open." Sam stared at Isaac in complete shock and horror, "WHAT...I can't do that!" Isaac's features hardened into a scowl. "Do you want to save Lum or not? That bird is not Lum; it is merely a vessel nothing more, but if you leave her in there she will die,...now TAKE IT!"

Sam took the knife and cut the binding around the boy then slammed it back into his hand. "You do it. I don't want to hurt her anymore." The boy's eyes turned even colder when he stood up placing the knife in Sam's hand then closed her fingers around it. "Isaac cannot harm a living creature plant nor animal, don't you understand he is a mix of a water sprite king and a wood sprite Priestess, if he were to hurt any living creature he would be banished from our world. He would be useless." This time Sam slapped the boy with no regrets.

Isaac crumbled to the floor holding his cheek. "How dare you he's your son are you just using him too?" Rowan rubbed Isaac's sore cheek. "Isaac doesn't understand how important he is, you have to show him. He is capable of so much. He can save the forest, he can free his people, and he can save Lum if you help him." Once again his arm reached out and his fingers closed around Sam's giving her the encouragement to do what she must. Sam looked from the dying bird to Isaac's hands cupped around hers.

"Fine." She freed her hand from Isaac's and swallowed hard before plunging the knife into the bird's small chest. A tiny red bead formed at the point of the knife. Sam hesitated. "Tell me why is it you are speaking through Isaac what happened to him?" Rowan's emerald eyes drifted away from the girl. "It was a long time ago…when I sealed Isaac within the god tree Gurrell I died there in Gurrell's roots. Part of my consciousness must have stayed with my son. Only under great stress was I able to influence him. I know we have met briefly before when he was scared or panicked. He thinks about you often Sam; that is why you must help him fulfill his destiny… and keep him from

it. Now stop stalling and do what you must to save Lum" Sam looked away from the boy and down to the small bird lying motionless in her hand; a small red line ran down the center…. "It is ok child she doesn't feel anything right now, but you need to hurry!" Sam pushed a little harder pulling the knife all the way down the bird's abdomen. There was no more blood. "Ok now what do I do?" Sam had thought that by some magic Lum would be released once she cut the bird open. The answer to her question was both unexpected and undesirable. "What do you mean 'now what' you must pull Lum's essences from the bird" Sam turned from Isaac to Lum. "How am I supposed to know what that is?" Rowan pushed Isaac's body up to be eye level with Sam. "Trust me child you won't be able to miss it, but you are going to have to open her chest."
Sam pushed the lump in her throat back down, and apologized once again as she dug her fingers past the soft feathers. The sound of a twig snapped as she pushed down on the bird's tiny rips. "I'm sorry Lum" she whispered so softly she could barely hear it herself. When she parted the

ribs a blue light shined from under the bird's lungs.

"Good it is still glowing. Go on child take it out" Sam peered over her shoulder at Isaac. Her hand shook and the knife hit the floor with a clatter. She could still feel the tears pulling at her eyes as she looked back down at the bird. "I'm really sorry." Clamping her eyes shut, she felt past the tiny velvet sacks of air until her fingers ran over a hard smooth pebble. She closed her fingers around it and plucked the tiny heart from its cage. Peering past her lashes, she stared down into the exposed chest of the dead bird in her hand. "Please forgive me Lum."

"I told you that bird is not Lum. You are holding what is left of her between your fingers."

Sam looked at the glowing blue stone and held it up. "What am I supposed to do with this, how does this save Lum?" Rowan lowered her voice into a gentle encouragement. "You have to swallow it before her light fades"

"WHAT!" Isaac stepped over to the girl, the Priestess voice murmuring through his lips, "Please forgive me for doing this to you my son,

but I will need to awaken that part of you which I
have kept asleep for so long."
Sam couldn't believe her eyes. The boy's body
started to glow as blue light danced through his
veins. He stood in front of her placing his hand
over the jewel and spoke in a tongue Sam had
never heard before. It sounded arcane and ancient.
The blue light pooled at his hand and shot into the
jewel; it began to pulse with a steady light.
Suddenly Isaac's body collapsed as the light
receded toward his chest. His breathing was
labored as he tried to speak. "Now Sam, she's
waiting." Sam stared down at the boy, it sounded
like his voice again. "Isaac?"
 The boy nodded then looked up with his usual
impish smile lighting up his light aqua colored
eyes. "It's ok you can save her now."
    The jewel was cold on her tongue; she
hesitated. "I can't believe I'm doing this." Isaac
merely nodded beckoning her with his hands to
go on; it was ok. Sam closed her eyes and popped
the small stone in her mouth. It was worse than
swallowing an ice cube whole. It melted on the
way down into a freezing liquid that filled her
lungs. She felt like she was drowning in that frigid

pool all over again, but this time there was no surface to paw for no place to escape the water's icy fingers. Air could not come to her fast enough it was if the water had replaced the air and there was no getting it back. Isaac ran to her side as she gasped for breath crumbling to the floor. "I'm sorry Sam I didn't know it would be this painful...but I know Lum would never try to hurt you."

Her body curled into a ball and started to shiver in his arms. Her lips paled. "I..c-c-c..a-an't..f-f-feel...my l..l..ee..ggs" Isaac look down her body, her legs had turned icy blue.

"Just hang in there ok,...I won't leave you." He pulled her to him rubbing her arms to warm them. "What's all the commotion eh?" The click of boots grew louder then suddenly stopped. A loud crash rattled the door. Isaac knew they were in danger, but he also knew his body was too weak from loss of blood and the ritual he had just performed on Lum. There wasn't much he could do right now. As long as Sam was like this he would have to carry her; and he didn't have the strength. He had told her that he would not leave her, so he held her body against his and waited.

277

A.J. Zanders

The lock clicked and the door knob turned; it creaked on its hinges as it opened. A man over six feet tall in a brown suit, which looked to be tailored just for him, stood in the doorway. Isaac blinked at the interloper a little confused. "You..." Sam rolled over slowly to see who Isaac was talking to. "Cat...you came back" His tall figure faded from her eyes and her breathing slowed to a shallow pace. "Sam!...Isaac what happened?" Isaac averted the man's anxious brown eyes and said nothing. Releasing a frustrated sigh, Lewie pinched the bridge of his nose between his fingers. "Look it doesn't matter, but we need to get her out of here." Lewie removed his coat and bent down to wrap it around Sam. Isaac would not relinquish his grip instead he pulled her closer.

"I'm just trying to help Isaac we need to get her to the hospital"

"No!"

His patience was wearing thin, "Listen that bump I gave Marco isn't going to keep him out forever we need get out of here!"

Isaac's sea-green eyes drifted down to Sam's pale arms and up to her spiked blonde hair. "Lum won't hurt her…I know she wouldn't." Lewie looked confused, "Lum?"

Isaac looked up with a eerie calm expression on his boyish face. "Yeah she's my Aunt; and Sam swallowed her heart."

"What!" Lewie's face twisted from confused to disturbed. Ignoring the outburst, Isaac stood up and handed Sam over to Lewie. "Here, take her back to my father."

"Your father, but how did you ….?" Isaac just pointed to the gaudy brown and orange suit. Blood flushed in the man's cheeks "Oh." Wrapping the coat around Sam, He held her securely to his chest and headed for the door. "Come on Isaac let's get out of here!" He stopped and turned back when he realized Isaac wasn't following him. "What are you waiting for? You don't want to stay here when Marco gets up do you?" Isaac stared at the six toes adorning each foot then his eyes drifted over to the plumb bags of purple liquid. The boy's expression appeared distant. "What difference does it make who uses me?"

Gently laying Sam down, Lewie walked over to Isaac. "Listen I don't really know your situation,

but people can only use you if you let them. And
by staying here you're letting Marco use you."
...Isaac pressed his hands into his ears as if the
screams of pain would return again. "Shut UP!
You have no idea what they ask of me!" Stunned
Lewie backed down, he never expected the kid to
be so passionate; he had always seemed so calm
almost stoic. It wasn't like Lewie to lose his temper
either, but now wasn't the time to save face.
"You're right I don't have a clue. What I do know
is that Sam cares for you and she came all this way
to help you and look what happened...now grow
up and be a man!" Isaac looked to the entire world
like he was going to burst into tears, but just as his
lip started to quiver it stopped. He turned around
gathering up all the bags of his blood he could
carry and hurried past Lewie. The tall human
grinned then scooped the girl back up and
followed after him.
"Wait!" Lewie stopped when Isaac's hand shot up.
"What is it?" He looked down as the boy pointed
to something; a tiny sprout had wiggled out of a
crushed acorn shell. "An acorn?" Isaac turned
grinning like a fool. "Yeah an acorn." Pulling the
antique knife from his pocket, he slit one of the

bags open and poured all the iridescent liquid onto the tiny seedling. Lewie couldn't believe his eyes it was incredible. The seedling quickly grew into a sapling and was getting taller and thicker by the minute.

"Come on" Isaac motioned that they should leave. Before the door could close on the new sapling Isaac gave the plant one last look, "Good luck."

A.J. Zanders

Ch. 20

"Our savior will be lost"

"You old fool" A bony hand brushed the fading pink and violet curls from the old woman's forehead "If only you could see me now you would have left me as a tree" She held her hand up to the morning sun the light shined through her paper thin skin. Examining the thick dark veins crossing over her knobby knuckles, she sighed. She whipped her hand from her sight at

the sound of a scream coming from the direction
of the park. "WISTERIA!"
The old sprite looked over from her sister as two
figures ran toward her. She blinked past copper
eyes at the three interlopers. Her eyes traveled
along the two boys then rested on the girl in the
man's arms. "So she was the one my sister spoke
of." Isaac looked from Sam's unconscious body to
the woman holding Wisteria. "Who are you?" The
old sprite patted the dirt beside her. "Come here
boy I assume you are what all the fuss is about."
Cautiously Isaac left Sam and Lewie's side. "What
happened to Wisteria?"
 Autumn ran the back of a withered hand down
the boy's cheek; a weak smile pulled at the corner
of her mouth. "She was a fool. She used a
forbidden ritual to bring me back. It was a job
meant only for the Prince, but alas she was too
tender hearted to sacrifice you for her own
personal motives." Isaac quickly pulled his cheek
from the old woman's touch and stared down at
Wisteria. "No! You can't say this is my fault."
Isaac reached down shaking the lifeless sprite.
"Wisty wake up, stop kidding I know I don't listen
to you, but I promise I will from now on…Please

Wisty!" Tears rolled down his face. Her still features cursed him. "It's not my fault….Wake up you stupid old goat!" He shook her harder.

"Isaac stop…please stop it!" He pulled his watery eyes from Wisteria to the familiar voice coming from the girl in Lewie's arms. "Sam?" Sam laid a gentle hand on Lewie's chest and smiled "You can put me down now Cat…I'm all right." He politely did as she asked. Sam walked over to the old woman and the boy. Resting her hands on his shoulders, she knelt down beside him. "Isaac it's ok. She didn't want to force you into this. She knew what it would cost you. She was just… bitter." Isaac looked a little perplexed, "How do you know that?" Smiling, she pointed towards her chest, "From Lum of course."

Sam turned from Isaac to face the old woman, her hand out stretched, "Hello Auntie…um we've never met, but I am your sister's daughter." Autumn smiled, "Yes my dear you are" Taking the girl's hand she pulled her into a tight embrace.

Feeling awkward and out of place Lewie scratched the back of his head and tried to find a considerate way to bring things back to their current situation. "I hate to break up such a warm reunion, but Marco does know where we are or at least an idea of where to search. I think we should move as far away from the park as possible."

Autumn pushed the girl away holding her at arm's length and nodded; "He's right my dear we should go toward the cave." Sam pulled away from her Aunt to look down at her mother. The old woman's breath had stopped; she looked so serene and fragile. "We can't just leave her here." Autumn patted her gently on the shoulder. "Don't worry child" she looked past Sam and beckoned for Lewie. "Come here lad you look like a nice strong young man...give an old lady a hand would you?"

Lewie blushed then nodded. He stepped over to the two sprites and gingerly picked up Wisteria's body.

"Now follow me" she commanded

The four walked deeper into the woods until they came to a wide circle of trees. In its center were the burnt remains of a large sycamore. "Lay her here please." Lewie carried Wisteria's body over to the burnt tree and laid her on the ground as the old sprite directed. "Now back up, unless you all want to be buried with her." Lewie lowered his head and stepped back to give Autumn room; everyone else did the same. Autumn stood before the fossil of the great sycamore; she motioned for Isaac to stand beside her. He reluctantly stepped up and stood silently beside her. "Now just do as I do boy and you'll be fine" … Autumn dropped down to her knees and placed her hands in the dirt, Isaac mimicked her movements without question. Silence fall among them as Autumn placed her forehead to her sister's and began humming. Isaac sat uncomfortably with his hands buried in the dirt near Wisteria's body. Autumn stopped humming when she realized the boy wasn't. "Well, catch up boy I can't do this alone." Isaac leaned down pressing his forehead to Wisteria's. He could feel her spirit, fiery and wild, as if he could capture it with his thoughts.

In unison the two spoke in a tongue that sounded much like the one Isaac used back at the club.

Please take care of our precious sister. Return her to a time when she was young and the woods were plentiful. Let her rest now in your heart.

Both Lewie's and Sam's jaws slacked as the ground beneath Wisteria's body opened up. Thin hairy roots bubbled up from the ground, surrounding the woman's body. Autumn stood up brushing the dirt from her knees. "Well if any of you have any last words for my crabby little sister...speak up!" She wiped a tear from her eye and stepped back. Sam hesitantly approached the edge of the grave. Leaning down; she arranged Wisteria's things neatly beside her, except the gourd, she knew it might be wrong, but it was all she had left of her mother. "I don't know why you gave me up, but I guess you are not a bad person after all. Just so you know I'm keeping this ok Mom." ...Lewie choose to stay back, being the only true human of the group, it just felt wrong to join them. Isaac continued to stare at the shallow grave as the young roots waved like grass around the old sprites body. Slipping the bracelet from his wrist, he placed it gingerly in her hands. "I'm sorry I was such a bad pupil Wisty...I hope you rest peacefully from now on." He took a step back as the fuzzy tendrils began wrapping around her body. Like the threads of a caterpillar into a chrysalis; the soft velvety threads merged and hardened. Autumn turned away wiping a tear from her eye. "She's a bit of a hard nut, but take care of her for me will you?"

Swallowing her own tears, Sam reminded the rest they had other bitter news to deliver. "Come on we should go tell Renlacir about Lum." Autumn looked up in shock, "Lord Ren...and princess Lumaria? You've met the water sprite king and his sister?" Sam turned back to Autumn and smiled, "yeah."

The morning light poured over the streets. It illuminated the remains of the Greek brother's dilapidated club; it crept further down the street to Club *Enchant*. Sprouting from its roof top was a full grown Oak tree. "Woooo...amazing simply amazing." Marco rubbed the sore spot at the back of his head. Staring up at the thick branches protruding from the windows, he grinned. "That is an impressive tree." He knelt down by the base and dipped his fingers into a small pool of an iridescent purplish liquid. A small plastic bag had been pierced by one of the smaller branches overhead. "Ah so my little golden goose cracked one of my eggs did he tsk tsk tsk...I guess I'll just have to squeeze that hen until it's nearly dry"

A wicked smile pulled at his lips as he navigated his way over the thick roots. "It's a good thing I know where my little bird roosts."

"Ren...Ren are you here?" Sam's voice echoed off the walls and across the water but, there was no sign of the water sprite. "Ren!"..."Where is he?"
Something made a wet flopping sound, it was subtle, but soon everyone heard it. The slap of wet flesh was muffled by a thick stalagmite near the pool. Everyone rushed to find a fish gasping for

breath as it struggled to get back into the water. "Ren?"

Sam and Isaac dove for him each trying to get him back into the pool. A loud bang reverberated throughout the cave, a muffled thumb followed. All eyes watched as Lewie's body hit the ground.

"Cat!" Sam ran to Lewie's side and pressed her hand into his wound.

"I should have done that from the beginning" Marco's voice resonated off the walls making his location difficult to pin point.

"Marco, you son of a bitch. Where are you?" Sam's eyes darting from one wall to the next.

"Astonishing, absolutely, astonishing." Clapping bounced off all the surfaces, but Sam didn't need sound to find him. Marco emerged in plain view right in front of the pond. "You do know some interesting people Sammie."

"How did you?"

"Let's not get into details Sammie. Let's just say you six... oh wait sorry, four are not the only ones of your kind..." He flashed his gold tipped teeth and fished in his jacket pocket; pulling forth what appeared to be a blade of grass. "You see my little informant told me exactly where to go." He twirled the blade between his fingers. "Thanks to you Sammie, if you hadn't left its counterpart at the club I wouldn't have been able to find this place... You see I picked its memory and found its brother just outside this cave." Sam's face twisted in shock.

"Surprised Sammie...what you thought you were the only one whose parents were different?" Fixing her gaze on Marco, she continued to press the wound in Lewie's side. "What are you talking about?" Marco glanced over at the pool then back toward Sam. "You see, my mother died giving birth to me. She was human so she was capable of carrying me 'til birth, but died the moment I was born; dried up like a prune." The blade in his hand crumbled between his fingers as he spoke. His face twisted as he laughed, "No matter how much water she drank it was never enough." Sam's eyes widened, "You mean?"

"That's right Sammie, my father was a water sprite, just like his...." He pointed his gun at Isaac. ".... you see water sprites can't stay away from a source of water for too long." Marco fired a few rounds at Isaac's feet causing him to jump back away from the flaying fish. Sam stared at the fish as it made a desperate attempt to get back in the water a shard of rock puncturing from its side. Marco turned swing the gun back at Sam as she tried to move toward Isaac. *BANG*

Sam felt the sharp sting as the bullet enter her shoulder and the force sent her stumbling backward to land beside Autumn.

"Stay there like a good girl Sammie....we could have made such a good team my chicka, but you had to take his side." He nodded his head at Lewie's body then waved the gun at Sam. "Hands up Sammie." Sam attempted to do as he commanded, but one arm refused to listen... "Aw what's the matter did I damage something important?"

Sam looked down at her limp arm bleeding from the shoulder; the bullet must have torn through her tendons; it just hung there useless

A wet slap on the ground brought everyone's attention back to the pool.

SPLASH

Before Marco could react Isaac and the fish were gone. "Damn it!" Marco hovered around the pool keeping the gun pointed at the water's surface while shouting instructions to the old sprite. "You old woman, take the girl away from that carcass before I put a bullet in you too!"

Autumn nodded at the man's back then pulled Sam further away from Lewie's body. "Come child it will be alright, Isaac has escaped."

Sam stared at the slow ebbs in the water and was reluctant to move…"You don't understand Marco is relentless he will catch him."…They could hear him goading the two in the water…"Come out come out my little golden goose and I promise not to hurt your friends eh!" He continued to pace the edge of the water waving his gun. …"Don't believe me do you?"

Marco swung his arm around towards Sam and Autumn and another bang rang throughout the cave. The rock shattered near Sam's head; particles of rock flew into the air penetrating her eye.

"Enough…if you want me then let them go!" Isaac's voice vibrated the water surface.

Turning toward the pool, Marco grinned maliciously. "Maybe I will maybe I won't. What if I refuse? I think I'd like to keep Sammie around…for a scrawny thing she's got some nice legs."

The water bubbled up and Isaac emerged a knife at his throat. "Let them go or your little golden goose is as good as dead!" …Marco pulled the gun from the girls and held his hands up slowly. "Easy now, let's work this out bambino."

Isaac looked at the two women huddled in the corner both trying to stop the bleeding from Sam's shoulder. "I will go with you if you let me escort them out of the woods." …Marco gave it some thought, and then waved for the boy to exit the pool and get in front of him. Isaac stepped out of the pool and over to the girls. Kneeling down, he reached out to help Sam up. Sam looked into his vivid blue eyes and marveled at the change in the boy's demeanor, "Isaac?"… He winked and his aquamarine orbs slid toward the large stalagmite. "Come on let's get out of here!" Isaac tugged her lightly by the arm. Then Sam felt the barrel of the gun wedge itself between her shoulder blades forcing her forward. "Move it!" Marco was clearly getting impatient to attain his prize. They all glanced briefly at the man's body lying on the ground. Sam was hesitating to move. "Cat…" "Poor Sammie you've already lost two friends today…be a good girl so you don't lose anymore, now move." Marco dug the barrel deeper into her back; it scorched her skin beneath her shirt. New hatred burned inside her. Her escorting sprites seemed to notice the girl's tension and stepped in between her and Marco. "We're going, just be sure to hold up your end of the deal." Isaac glared at the Sicilian.

Marco narrowed his eyes at the boy; something seemed off, before the wheels were allowed to turn too far Autumn spoke up. "Come on dears he might change his mind if we don't do as he says." She tugged on the girl's arm and encourage Isaac to do the same.

The sun had risen above the tree tops an almost blinding light greeted them as they stood at the edge of the forest. "That's far enough we don't need witnesses now do we?" Marco waved his gun between them as if debating who to shoot first, then there was a loud bang. Sam spun around just as Isaac dove in front of the muzzle pointed at Autumn. "Isaac!" Dropping down to her knees, she cradled him in her arms. "Isaac hold on! I'm sure Ren could fix this."

Warm liquid seeped on to her lap; it felt like so much blood, but she did not dare lose eye contact with Marco to look down.

"Now that's just great you've gone and made me shoot the wrong person!" Annoyed he pointed the gun at Sam's head then swung over to Autumn's. "Which bitch should I shoot first?"…Anger rose to replace her fear and Sam shouted "Marco you bastard I suggest you shoot me first because if you don't, you will regret it." A crooked smile pulled on his face filling his half crazed eyes. He swung the gun around to rest in Sam's directions. "I will miss you my chicka."

The hammer clicked. Shutting her eyes, she clung to Isaac for her last bit of comfort. A moment past and nothing happened. She peered past her lashes to find Marco was gone. Scanning the park, her gaze fell on a green mass being pulled into the woods. Sam shot a look toward Autumn, who shook her head denying any claim. "It's ok now, we're safe." She did her best to give the girl a comforting smile. Sam turned from the old woman to the boy in her lap; his blue eye's drifting closed. "Isaac...Isaac don't you dare leave me like this...Damn you!"

He smiled and reached up to wipe a tear from her cheek, "You have such a bad memory Samantha."

"Ren?"

His body burst like a water balloon. The warm liquid had not been blood at all, but essentially Ren's disguise slipping as he lost consciousness. All that was left was the soaked clothing he had been wearing. "Ren!"

Sam scurried to scoop as much of the water into a puddle as she could before it all seeped into the ground..."Quickly child, grab something living anything a frog a lizard anything", Autumn commanded.

There was nothing to save him; most of the smaller creatures had been frightened off by all the commotion. "There isn't anything" Sam watched in horror as the last of the water vanished beneath the soil. "Ren!...No! I'm Sorry Ren...Damn it" Pounding her fist into the ground, she could not stop the tears from rolling down her cheeks. She had lost three in one day, the pain overwhelmed her. "Damn it Marco this is all, your fault!" she shouted then launched herself into the woods after him.

"No child you mustn't you'll only cause him trouble!" Autumn called out to stop her, but Sam could only hear the swish of anger-fueled blood in her ears. "Come back here you coward, so I can beat the crap out of you!" Sam yelled.

Pushing her legs harder, she chased the captive Sicilian as he zipped through the trees. She ran so far she could no longer hear Autumn shouting for her to return. "Alright Marco where are you?" …Something moved in her peripheral vision. She turned to face what looked like a massive nest of serpents, wiggle beneath a towering maple. Two long green velvet ropes shot out from the mass and attached themselves to the trunk, and then began to haul their prey up the tree.

Sam ran to it.

"What are you doing here Sam….Leave!" She froze as Isaac's voice shot from behind the Maple…"Isaac?"

"Leave Sam before you get hurt!" Isaac emerged from behind the trunk; his sea-green eyes held nothing but hatred. As he stepped toward Sam the vines around Marco tightened. Sam could here Marco gasping for breath…. "Isaac I know he's a jerk, but you shouldn't sink to his level!"

Isaac remained silent his face giving no indication she had gotten through…"Please Isaac what about what your mother said about harming another living creature!"

Isaac glanced over to Sam; his eyes softened slightly then hardened again. "So what if I am useless afterward… then I can live a normal life. You heard what she said; I'd be useless, no good to the forest…" Isaac flung a slender finger toward Marco, "…. and no good to him."

It was true and it was tempting to let Isaac go through with it, but something in her heart told her there was more to this bond of sprite and creature; that something terrible would happen; something beyond just the loss his power.

Stop him, Lum's voice rang throughout Sam's skull. *He doesn't understand he will not only lose his power over the flora and fauna he will wither and die slowly, painfully and no one would be able to stop it!*

…Sam's eyes widened; before she knew it she had wrapped her arms around him. "Please Isaac I don't want you to die you mustn' do this, he is beneath you!"

The ropes around Marco slackened allowing him to breathe again. He took the opportunity to speak, not wanting anything to happen to his golden goose. "Hey kid, you might want to listen to her…" Sam and Isaac turned to find Marco had freed his face and his left hand. "….thanks for stalling my chicka… "

He placed his free hand on the vine and it withered into dry crispy ropes…"Ah now that felt good." Marco stepped away from the tree readjusting his jacket and resetting his rings. "You see I may not be as talented as you two, however I still have a pretty useful trick up my sleeve." Reaching out, he placed his hand on the trunk of the Maple. Leaves showered down around them, branches shattered like glass, and then the trunk itself snapped in half crashing to the ground. A wicked smile tugged at his lips. "Now that's what I call a meal."

Isaac and Sam stood flabbergasted.

"You see you'll have to do better than a few vines
my little golden goose."
Isaac grabbed Sam's arm and pulled. "Come on!"
Snatching two plastic pouches from the ground,
he punctured them allowing his blood to speckle
the earth behind them as they ran. Bushes, tall
grass, and vines grew rapidly to block Marco's
path; each one ended in the same fate, dry, brown
and lifeless.
"This is a useless game Chicka just give up."
Marco taunted behind them. Sam glanced over her
shoulder as the forest began to wither at Marco's
touch. "Isaac he's right we can't keep this up."
"No you can't"
Whipping around, Sam found Lewie standing
ankle deep in the creek next to a large black bear.
"Lewie? Cat? Is that really you….You're ok." She
wanted to cry again. Lewie smiled, "Yeah thanks
to that little miracle worker there." he said
pointing towards Isaac. Isaac blushed.
"Now let's take care of Marco shall we?" He held
up a match in one hand and Wisteria's gourd in
the other. A dripping rag hung from its neck. "No
Lewie don't it's all I have of my mother now!"
Lewie turned his eyes from Sam. "I'm sorry Sam,

but Isaac and I don't see any other way." He looked at Isaac, who nodded. Isaac swung Sam into the creek just as Lewie loped the flaming gourd toward Marco.

"Isaac! No it's not what you think Lewie is…" Sam tried to stop him but was held firm by two enormous furry arms ending in long yellow claws. "Let me go Koda…Isaac!"… Stopping briefly he turned back to her. "Take care, Sam." He looked from the bear to Lewie, "Koda…Lewie…get her out of here!" …Sam struggled against her captives, "No Isaac what are you doing? You'll die!" Isaac did not turn around this time; Sam watched the elfin figure as he was swallowed by the flames. "Let me go damn it…he'll die out there *cough*" "Sam we'll all die out here if we don't leave now" Lewie pried her from the bear's claws and tossed her over his shoulder. She kicked and screamed as he carried her down the creek. "Please let me go Lewie, he doesn't think anyone loves him; he thinks everyone just wants to use him. I have to let him know he's wrong, please!" Tears soaked through Lewie's shirt as she buried her face into his back.

"Don't worry Sam he knows."

cough cough

Isaac navigated through the smoke, heading back toward the colony of trees gathered around Gurrell. He knew sprites were there, if he was going to start some place it mine as well have been where it all started. They had asked for his help before, this time he wasn't going to run away. "So you think you can save them do you?"...Isaac spun around to find Marco; steam was emanating from his body. Ash had settled on his face making his gold capped teeth stand out against his blackened lips. He leaned on a nearby tree; it too withered at his touch. "I'll just have to keep stealing their moisture until I come across someone important to you, unless of course you are willing to be my slave."

Another tree shriveled up under Marco's touch, and then was quickly consumed by the flames.

"So what now boy, there are a lot of trees in this forest, some of them might contain your precious people…" He flexed his hand. "…I could keep this up for a while; so long as I can steal their essence this fire cannot hurt me."

Isaac watched as Marco sucked the life from another tree it too burst into flames. The boy's features hardened into an assiduous resolve.

"Then, I'll just have to beat you to them!"

"Lewie put me down!" Sam pounded her fist into Lewie's back, but he refuse to set her down. Once they reached the clearing he placed her on the ground, but kept a firm grip of her hand. He wanted to make sure she didn't try to go back in after Isaac.

"Psst over here" …Outside the forest Autumn stood waiting; a bundle of wet clothing draped in her arms. "Where is Isaac?" she asked the two as they emerged covered in soot and ash. Her eyes traveled from their dreary faces to a cloud of smoke rising from the center of the forest. "Oh my...he isn't still in there is he?" Lewie looked at Sam and she looked at him neither could form the words. Stepping up to the frail sprite, Koda growled softly then leaned on her for comfort. "I see." she understood what the bear needed and why. Reaching down, she patted the bear's head. "Despite that woman's effort it was all for not." She lowered her head shaking it. "I suppose there is no way to escape one's destiny."

Tearing her eyes from the old woman, Sam gazed desperately into the forest. "Please be ok Isaac." Thousands of gallons of water rushed into the trees past Sam and Lewie. Half a dozen fire trucks and police cars pulled into the parking lot. Everyone was doing their best to keep the fire from spreading into the city.

Throwing Isaac's wet shirt over Samantha's head, Autumn ushered them out of the park. "Come on dears we should leave before they suspect we are the cause of this." Sam hugged the wet shirt around her...it still smelt like Isaac even wet. The further they walked away from the forest the more it hurt. "Lewie we can't leave him in there."

Attempting to free herself, Sam tried to make a break for the woods. Lewie quickly wrapped his arm around her waist. "Sorry Sam."… She felt his warm breath on her ear then a sharp pain to the back of her neck. The world faded in a haze of black smoke.

A.J. Zanders

Ch. 21

"A new life will be born"

The fire had crawled inside Isaac's lungs, restricting his air flow, his chest tightened, his eyes burned. He had lost Marco in the smoke. He knew the forest better than anyone, but still he would not be able to go on for much longer. He had to find the remaining sprites. Rising out of the smoke were two twisted pear trees, their smooth bark charred black. A soft echo pleaded in his mind, "Free us…it hurts!"

Isaac pushed up his sleeves and pressed his palms to the singed bark. "Can you hear me?"… "Yes…who are you?" echoed again like stereo inside his skull. "It doesn't matter, if you can understand me then open your soul to me I can get you out of there."… "Do what?"… "Well that is a rather odd thing to ask" The two voices bounced back and forth inside his head, he thought he was going to go crazy. "Please, just trust me!"… "Um okay"… "If it will get us out of here, sure."

Closing his eyes, Isaac concentrated until he could feel their heartbeat match his own. Focusing his energy into his hands; they began to glow with a green light. He pushed his essences into the bark. The thin shapes began to mold into lumpy figures that grew arms and legs. When Isaac opened his eyes two small boys held each of his hands. "It is nice to meet you sir. …Where are we?"… "Yes and where is our village? Do you know how to get back there? "… "Yes this stuff is dreadfully painful." Isaac's head rocked back and forth as one twin asked one question synced with the other. This was too much. "I don't know what village you are talking about, but you need to get out of here… go north you'll find a cave." The twins looked at each other and nodded "K" "See you mister."

Once free of the twins Isaac moved on to locate others. His skin began to tingle and burn. Looking down he could see the color had darkened, it felt stiff and itchy. A hard plate of bark had formed a patch on his arm where Marco had grabbed him back at the club.

"Come on boy you and I could make a fortune *cough* no need to be irrational what do you owe this forest anyway?" Unbelievable, Marco was still able to find him. He was barely standing as he leaned on one tree after another; his body was starting to fall apart. His fingers were merged into a paddle, and his features were blurry. "I see that little mark I left is causing you some trouble, let's be rational adults, boy… Tell you what I'll share the profits. You and Sammie could live a happy life in the city…you'd like that wouldn't you?" Isaac turned away, but for a moment his steps faltered. It was true he would give anything to live like a human in the city with Sam, but not like that. He was far from forgiving this man. The ground around Marco's feet caved; roots and vines shot up wrapping around his shoulders. They pulled him in like the prey of a giant squid. There were too many for him to fend off. Marco pawed at the roots attempting to drain the water from them in order to escape. Surprised, Isaac stood gapping like a fish. Had he done that? A deep smooth voice penetrated his thoughts, shaking him from his trance. *Go child! I will not let you hurt another; I will take care of this half breed human.* "Who are you?" *I was once called Elder Sequoia, but it doesn't matter any longer, now hurry child go to the others.*

Gasping and coughing, Marco fought for air as his breath was gradually squeezed from his body. "Bambino!" … Isaac tore his eyes from the tree to the man in its clutches. Struggling to speak, Marco pleaded, "Will you let ….a fellow half sprite, like yourself…die here? … We could both leave here…a… alive!"

Isaac stared once more at the ancient tree; he had not been the one to trap the human, but was not helping just as bad? "Please Elder Sequoia let him go!"

Son of Rowan…you must hurry the forest is in danger, this man is not worth your time.

Small trees burst like fire crackers around them. The massive tree began to sizzle as steam rose from its bark. Marco's body started to shrivel and burn within its roots. Without thinking Isaac dove to free him. The man's skin peeled and floated away like burnt paper. Reaching out, Isaac took hold of Marco's hand, it scorched his palm. Alarmed, he jerked back. Marco was actually still trying to drain him "Please boy just a little!" …Unable to free himself of the fear Isaac backed away as he watched the Sicilian's body crumbled into ash.

I know what you are feeling child, but I assure you, this man deserved what just happened to him. He has finally repaid his debt to the forest. Now boy, go free others.

"What about you?" Pulling back his sleeves Isaac pressed his palm into the trunk.

What are you doing boy? Leave me! I am tainted now, you should not free me!

"There he is!" a voice shouted through the smoke. "Yes, you have to come with us!"…Isaac turned from the tree to find the twins running in

313

his direction. "What are you doing, go back to the cave!" "But we found someone!" "Yes, someone soft!" … "Come" "Follow, Follow"

It is all right child, leave me. The twins wrapped their bony fingers around Isaac's wrist and hauled him away from the Elder tree. The boys drug him through the woods. It hurt to breath and his limbs felt stiff; each step he took sent small tendrils searching the ground for a place to root. His attempt to free Marco and the Elder took more out of him then he realized. The twins finally stopped pulling on Isaac's arms when they came to break in the forest. "Looky Looky"… "See we told you we found somebody."

The ground was scorched black. Standing in the middle, was a young sapling sycamore. The smoke here had created a low ceiling amongst the trees. As they approached Isaac could make out the towering black figure of Gurrell and the now black remains of Wisteria's grave.

"See…she's cute isn't she?" … "If you say so"… "What do you mean? …Of course she is!" … Isaac pushed past the twins as they argued. "She?" The ground beneath their feet trembled. … *Save her…Protect her… we will give her our lives…just*

314

save her. Roots rushed towards the small sapling, from the surrounding trees. As their roots made contact, the trees began to wither. "Stop you're killing yourselves!" ... *She fell from Gurrell's branches not long ago we have been feeding her...We were surprised, Gurrell must have placed the last of his energy into that seed. We think it was your touch...*

Stepping forward, Isaac placed his hands around the narrow trunk of the young tree. It was warm; he could feel its pulse beneath his palms. A gentle whisper spoke to his mind. Isaac nodded. "I understand. I'm sorry but you are the last one. I am very tired." His hands began to glow as he pushed his blood into the tree with is right hand and siphoned the sap with the other. His left arm stiffened; the patch on his forearm grew; it consumed his arm, then his shoulder. Panic raced through him as he watched the bark start to take over his body. He could feel the tree's pulse spike to match his. Sap raced through his veins to dump into his heart; sending it speeding through his entire body. He fell to his knees with a scream of pain. The roots of the other trees shot over to help him. The stress to his heart was too much; the other trees did what they could to help steady it.

Fear caused his palpitations to quicken. The
encroaching roots only served to feed his fear.

"Thank you." the voice was calm and gentle.
Isaac opened his eyes to a little girl with bright
agate colored eyes. Staring up at his quizzical face,
she smiled. She placed her hand over his heart and
hummed slow and gentle. "hmm I will protect
you…mmmm….grow strong….mmm." She
stepped back as his pulse had slowed to the
rhythm of her hum and the pain in his chest
seemed to have subsided.
"Didn't I tell you, Porty, you have to form a trust
first, still so foolish. But I suppose you have
earned a name for yourself haven't you?" She
leaned back as the bark continued to spread
through his body. "I suppose Woody is just as bad
as Porty….Well, seen as how you like it so much
you've earned the right to keep it…Isaac."
Smiling, he closed his eyes as he allowed the trees
to have him. "Take care of Sam for me."

Soft furry tentacles shot out from his feet and
buried themselves deep into the soil. They grew
thicker pulsing with the life of the forest as they
stretched up Isaac's legs and spread throughout
his entire body. Within minutes Isaac's skin had

turned to bark. His wooden armor reached higher until it sprouted into a massive green canopy.

The small sprite's bright yellow eyes traveled up into the brilliant green foliage then past them into a swirl of grey clouds. In a great crack the sky ripped open. The city had never seen so much rain. The girl smiled patting the trunk of the enormous tree. "You've done well Prince Isaac, your 'aunt' is very proud of you."
"Hey over here!" She turned her agate jewels from the magnificent tree toward two boys waving at her. "Hurry we found shelter!"

She bowed her depart to the sycamore, "We'll met again my prince you have much work to do."

A.J. Zanders

Epilogue

It had been six months since the fire. Spring had reclaimed the forest's charred remains, turning it into a beautiful painting of green, purple and yellow. The black oily figures poking through the light green foliage was a visual reminder of what happened all those months ago.

Sam knelt down in front of a large hollow oak filled with Isaac's treasures. It was crawling with purple flowered vines.

"Well, I think you'd be happy to see everything is growing so well after the fire." She set a white paper bag with pink lettering down beside the hollow. "I brought your favorite…oatmeal…I

made them myself. Lyna's a great teacher."
Releasing a heavy sigh, she fell back on her arms.
"Isaac you're a complete idiot!" Sam tossed her
head back to look up into the spring foliage as
new buds formed along the skinny branches. She
couldn't help but wonder if there had been a way
to prevent all of it.

"You knew didn't you Lum? You knew this was
how he would go?...I'm sorry I couldn't do
anything to prevent it." Holding her hand over
her heart, she could feel the cool essence of the
water sprite pumping through her veins.

*There was nothing you could have done Samantha.
No one wanted it to happen, not even Wisteria....*
Lum's voice went silent for a moment, before she
started again. *I'm sorry Samantha; you finally got
to meet your mother only to have her ripped away
again. I wish I had foreseen what that old fool had
planned. But alas ever since I was trapped in that
bird's body; I have been unable to see the future.*
Sam closed her eyes and squeezed her fingers
lightly over her chest. "It's ok Lum...I'm sorry
about your brother too, but at least that bastard
Marco paid for what he did to ever one."

"It was a relief when the police report said they found his rings and a positive match to his gold teeth amongst the charred remains. Thankfully it was all blamed on a lit cigarette."

Sam sighed and looked down at the many purple flowers that were her mother's namesake, then into the woods, before saying her goodbyes. "Well we'd better get back; it's my turn to watch the counter. I'll see you later mom keep watch while I'm away ok?"

I think she was happy back then, just being able to see you walk by once in a while was good enough for her.

"Do you think she can still sense things through the trees?"

I do

Sam smiled, "I think so too"

"It's this one" chimed a tiny voice….."It's this one", chirped another. …"No, it's this one" another voice said matter of factly.

"Yes, I do believe it is this one" the taller of the four agreed while patting the massive sycamore tree. Its canopy spread so high and wide that it nearly blocked out the sun.

"How do you know?" the first voice asked. "Yes, how do you know?" the second little voice adding to the first. "Come on tell us" the two resounded together.

Bright blue eyes looked from the two fuzzy blonde heads, over to the somber yellow eyes of the only girl in their group, then up into the branches and smiled,

"I think I know my son when I see him."

{The End….?}

LaVergne, TN USA
07 January 2011
211424LV00001B/1/P